D0387892

Dallas Public Library
950 Main Street
Dallas, Oregon 97338

FINDING LOVE
FOREVER

Other books by Shelley Galloway:

The Love Letter

The *Finding Love* Romance Series:

Finding Love for Lindsay
Finding Love Again
Finding Love in Payton
Finding True Love
Finding Love's Future
Finding Love's Fortune

FINDING LOVE FOREVER

●

Shelley Galloway

AVALON BOOKS
NEW YORK

© Copyright 2007 by Shelley Sabga
All rights reserved.
All the characters in this book are fictitious,
and any resemblance to actual persons,
living or dead, is purely coincidental.
Published by Thomas Bouregy & Co., Inc.
160 Madison Avenue, New York, NY 10016

Library of Congress Cataloging-in-Publication Data

Galloway, Shelley.
   Finding love forever / Shelley Sabga.
      p. cm.
   ISBN-13: 978-0-8034-9843-3 (acid-free paper)
   I. Title.
   PS3607.A42F5565 2007
   813'.6—dc22
                                        2007011964

PRINTED IN THE UNITED STATES OF AMERICA
ON ACID-FREE PAPER
BY HADDON CRAFTSMEN, BLOOMSBURG, PENNSYLVANIA

33049310 6/07

To Erin Niumata, who gave me such a thrill
the first time we talked . . . and has been a wonderful
editor and inspiration for the last seven years.
Thank you for letting me dream big dreams,
and make up a town called Payton.

Dallas Public Library
950 Main Street
Dallas, Oregon 97338

Chapter One

Daphne Reece carefully placed two cups of coffee on a tray right next to two perfectly proportioned slices of chocolate almond cake. After smoothing out the crease in her new baby blue linen slacks, she expertly carried the tray into the living room.

Jim was there, reading the paper, his legs propped up on an old ottoman that he'd refused to let her recover. The news was on, but on mute, which was good, since Jim had put on his favorite classical station, too. Strands of Schubert flowed in the air.

Daphne fought back a groan. She and Jim had replayed this scene a hundred times in a row. She could practically predict what each of them would say before they said the words. Though she usually found comfort in their routines, lately she'd been guilty of wishing there was a little spontaneity in their lives.

Maybe today was the day?

Summoning up a smile, she said, "Here we go, Jim. Two cups of coffee and dessert. I made the cake this afternoon."

Jim didn't look up.

After placing the tray on the coffee table, Daphne sat on the edge of it, taking care that her new white linen blouse was far from the chocolate frosting. Remembering how Jim used to say she was more tempting than any chocolate treat, she poufed up her hair a little bit. "Ready for dessert, darling?"

"Hmm."

The newspaper crackled as he turned the page. The soothing sounds of Schubert only seemed to taunt her. "Jim? Jim! Are you ever going to put that paper down and look at me?"

He folded the sheets in three quick movements. Blue eyes, so like their son Kevin's, looked her over. "There. Now what am I supposed to see?"

Me! She wanted to scream. But instead, she merely sighed. There'd been a time, oh, twenty or twenty-five years ago, when he'd only had eyes for her. He'd make a big fuss over her new clothes.

He'd be surprised and pleased when she made him a cake. He'd say all kinds of things to make her cheeks heat and her toes curl.

Now it was obvious he found her far less interesting than the newest linebacker on the Dallas Cowboys. And, she knew for a fact that he didn't even like the Cowboys!

Shifting her weight, Daphne gestured to the tray next to her. "Look at the cake. Isn't it lovely? I toasted the almonds before I arranged them around the edge. I think it looks good enough to serve at a dinner party. Don't you?"

His paper rustled. "I'll take the coffee, but I'm not too hungry, Daphne. I'll skip the cake."

That was it? She worked all afternoon to make him the cake, cleaned herself up before he got home from the office, and brought him coffee and dessert to his chair and . . . that's what she got? *I'll take the coffee and skip the cake?*

Right before her eyes, he took the cup she offered, sipped, and opened the blasted paper again.

He might as well have walked away.

Standing up, Daphne crossed the room to the mantle. There, in beautiful silver frames, were pictures of her children. Of their children. One was Christmas photo from when all the kids still lived at home. Another showed them all crowding around Missy and Kevin on their wedding day. A third highlighted Mary Beth and Cameron on their daughter Maggie's birthday. The fourth and fifth were of Joanne and Jeremy and their families.

Daphne knew she should be happy. All five children were married and had their own lives. They'd grown up to be independent, considerate people. She should be proud. She should be relieved. Now she and Jim could do all the things they'd never had time for in the past. Travel. Volunteer.

Learn Russian. She'd always wanted to learn an exotic language.

Unfortunately, sometime over the last dozen years they'd drifted apart, developing separate interests, communicating less and less.

Now she wasn't sure what they had, other than a good marriage. At least, she hoped it was a good one.

Looking back at her husband, Daphne pursed her lips. Why, she could practically be running around the house naked and he wouldn't notice! Not that she would ever do such a thing.

Crossing the room again, Daphne took her usual seat next to him. "I was thinking I'd make chili for everyone on Sunday night. It's been forever since I've made it, and the kids always liked my recipe. What do you think?"

"Sure, hon."

She tapped her foot. "Then, on Saturday night, I thought that we could go to the club. They're having a prime rib special."

"If you want."

Daphne was getting more than a little irritated. Peevishly, she picked up her own dessert from the tray and took a giant bite. The rich chocolate exploded in her mouth, making her feel almost happy.

But, as she looked at Jim again, she realized the feeling wasn't enough. Chocolate just wasn't going to cut it. She needed attention, she needed it from Jim, and she needed it that minute.

"Jim, dear, we need to talk." She set her plate down as she heard the desperation in her voice. Even to her own ears, she sounded like a woman on the edge!

Ever so slowly, his paper lowered again. "What do we need to talk about?"

Wasn't it obvious? "Us, Jim. We need to talk about us."

Jim picked up his cup and sipped. "Us?"

"I have a feeling that things just aren't good between us. Something's gone missing in our marriage. Jim, we're in a rut."

An eleven appeared in between his eyebrows, a sure sign he was annoyed. "Our 'rut' is called thirty-five years of marriage. It's called five kids, five independent kids who have their own lives. You're just sad they don't need you right now. You're lonely, Daphne."

So what if she was? Shouldn't he want to pick up the entertainment slack? "We see the kids a lot." Attempting to get him to understand, she said, "Jim, I'm missing the spark you and I used to have."

"Spark?" Jim started laughing. "Daphne, we're in our late fifties."

"We're not dead." She poufed her hair again, just to show him she could still be attractive.

He didn't notice. "We don't need to be sparking. We've sparked plenty of times."

"Not lately."

With a chuckle, he finally looked at her from head to toe. Like he used to. "You still are the prettiest girl I know, Bunny."

Bunny! He hadn't called her that pet name in years. Against her will, Daphne felt her cheeks heat. "So why is it that all you want to do now is sit around and read your paper?"

Like a flash, his amorous look was gone. "Daphne, I worked all day."

She stood up. It was time to do some thinking. Just because they'd been married thirty-five years didn't mean she had to look forward to an eternity of newspapers and Schubert.

She didn't even like classical music!

In a huff, she announced, "I'm leaving. I have an appointment. Someone answered Lindsay Bennett's ad about the apartment for rent."

Finally (*finally*) Jim looked interested in what she had to say. "Who do you think would be interested in living above a theater?"

"Someone named Virginia Young."

"Are you going to tell her that some people think it's haunted?"

She hadn't planned on it. "That little detail has never been proven."

Jim laughed. "But there's enough personal accounts to make us all sit up and take notice."

"In any case, I should be back in about an hour. Maybe even less."

But the sports section was plastered once again over his face. "S' okay."

Tapping the toe of her new powder blue mule, she said, "Actually, I might be late. I might go meet a younger man and flirt outrageously!"

"Have a good time, dear."

Daphne Reece narrowed her eyes. This would not do. Something drastic needed to be done. And she would do it, too, as soon as she figured what needed to be done. She didn't know when . . . but sometime soon, Jim Reece was in for a bumpy ride.

* * *

From the moment Ginny Young arrived in Payton, Ohio, she'd felt as if she'd come home. Payton had a good kind of homey feel to it. Rolling hills, quaint wooden clapboard houses. There was even a river flowing through the middle. The whole town felt welcoming and friendly, and especially now in early May.

Every business in downtown had a flower box filled with geraniums. The two restaurants she could see each had outside patios, filled with families and couples eating their dinner. A lone runner zipped past on the bike trail.

It was as far away from where Ginny had grown up that she could imagine.

She'd visited Payton before, several times. Once she'd even toured the area with a realtor. Unfortunately, the homes and duplexes were beyond her reach. She had just accepted the reality that Payton would always be beyond her means when she'd spied the ad in Sunday's *Payton Registrar.*

Quaint one bedroom apartment, conveniently located downtown. Price negotiable. Immediate occupancy.

It sounded just about perfect. The only thing that would hold her back would be if Mrs. Reece, the woman she was meeting, required more than the standard first and last months' rent.

Looking up at the front of the historic redbrick theater, Ginny hoped the lady would get there soon.

"Virginia? Virginia Young? I'm Daphne Reece."

"Hello. I'm Ginny." Her step faltered as she saw the lady walking toward her. Meticulously dressed in a linen blouse and sky blue slacks, Mrs. Reece looked like she would be highly selective when it came to tenants.

"I'm sorry I'm late," Mrs. Reece said in a rush. "I had a little trouble getting out of the house. I hope I haven't kept you waiting long?"

"Oh, no. I got here early."

"Well, you ready to see the apartment?"

With a nod, Ginny followed the other woman into the Sally McGraw Theater. "This is a rather old building," Daphne explained. "But it underwent an extensive renovation a little over two years ago. Now it's a terrific mixture of modern innovation and beautiful woodwork." She looked over her shoulder as Ginny pressed her palm against an intricately carved spindle on the stairwell. "My son-in-law did remodeled every inch of this place. Isn't he talented?"

Ginny tried to keep her expression nonchalant

as she spied the many other elaborate columns and woodwork that decorated the foyer. This place was going to cost a fortune to rent, she was sure of it. "It's pretty."

"Yes! Yes, it is." Motioning her toward a dark hallway, she said, "There's a little door over here that would be your entrance. You could enter, then lickety-split, be upstairs in no time."

Lickety-split? "That sounds great."

"You did hear that it was for a top floor apartment, didn't you?"

"Yes, ma'am."

"Good." They trudged on. "I, personally, enjoy climbing two flights of stairs on a regular basis." Patting a trim thigh, she whispered. "It keeps me in shape."

Ginny didn't dare look at the lady's leg. "The stairs are no problem."

"Good!" After pulling out a rather ornate skeleton key, Mrs. Reece unlocked the door. "Well, here it is, dear."

To Ginny's eye, the apartment looked a lot like a Barbie Dream House. Built-ins were everywhere, and every piece on a slightly smaller scale than she was used to. The kitchen was cute, the white appliances gleamed against the matching cabinets. All of it contrasted nicely with the gleaming wood floors.

"I made sure the place was spic and span earlier today."

"It's beautiful."

"I'm glad you like it. Why, it's just the perfect place to be all cozy. Lindsay, the gal who just moved out, loved it. So did my daughter Denise." With a wink, Mrs. Reece said, "Both girls got engaged while living here."

"That's something." Ginny couldn't imagine getting engaged anytime soon. Of course, maybe that's because it had been years since she dated seriously?

For some reason, Daphne suddenly looked melancholy. "Yes, before I knew it, I was planning weddings and organizing receptions. Now, they're happily married."

They looked around a few more minutes, then walked back down the stairs, Mrs. Reece describing the woodwork, the trim, the carpenter named Ethan Flynn, and finally her daughter Denise, who used to live in California but now lived in a cozy bungalow several blocks away.

Actually, by the time they reached the ground floor, Ginny was sure she knew more about the Reece family from this one petite woman than she knew about anyone else.

Finally, Daphne Reece spoke of the theater, how Denise and her friend Lindsay produced plays three times a year in the building, and how that affected the rent. Then, she told Ginny how much the rent would be.

It was about a hundred dollars less than what Ginny had hoped. In short, the place was a steal.

After Mrs. Reece locked the door behind them, she led Ginny to a nearby bench. "So, what did you think about the apartment?"

"It's very nice," Ginny hedged, doing her best to keep her voice neutral. It was a struggle. What she really wanted to do was clap and yell and say that she couldn't wait to move in.

"To my way of thinking, I believe it's a good deal, too. I did some research, and I think the rent we're charging is very reasonable."

Ginny struggled to keep from praising it too much. She wanted to be as cool and professional as she possibly could. "It is reasonable. Uh, did you want any money besides the first and last months' rent? A security deposit?"

"Gracious, no. Just knowing a real person is going to be inhabiting it is enough for me."

"A real person?"

For the first time in their short acquaintance, Daphne Reece seemed at a loss for words. "Ginny, um, I suppose I should let you know that they are some people in our town who have been spreading rumors that the theater might be haunted."

Now Ginny was struggling to keep her expression neutral for a whole different reason. She couldn't believe someone in this day and age would actually believe in such things. "Haunted by what?" she asked, playing along. The last thing she wanted to do was offend the one person who was going to help her finally live in Payton.

"A ghost. Sally McGraw." Daphne's eyes widened as she snapped her manicured fingers. "Quite honestly, I've never heard of her haunting the apartment, only the theater and foyer."

"What do you mean by haunt?"

"Well, I've never seen her in action. However, my daughters have told me on very good authority that Sally has an inordinate fondness for turning on stereos and opening windows." After a moment, she patted Ginny's arm. "But don't worry. I'm sure you'll be just fine."

If Ginny wasn't so determined to live in Payton, she'd be running. Either the theater was haunted . . . or Mrs. Reece was nuts. Neither sounded good.

Daphne pursed her lips. "When Denise and Lindsay lived here, they never mentioned anything spooky happening in the apartment." Giving Ginny a sly wink, she said, "Maybe she doesn't care for stairs like we do?"

Ginny was trying to figure out the answer to that one when a police officer wandered by.

"Hi Mrs. Reece," he said. Dressed in a blue t-shirt, khakis, and a belt that held police garb, he looked fit and handsome and way too close. "What are you doing out this way?"

"I'm showing the apartment above the theater. It's been vacant way too long."

"Ah."

As he turned to eye her, Ginny struggled to act like she didn't care he was standing with them. She'd never met a police officer she trusted, and didn't want to start now. Not even a police officer with olive skin, dark brown hair and eyes that reminded her of chocolate bars.

Daphne had already hopped up and hugged him. "It's been ages since we've seen each other, Luke." With a flourish, she gestured toward Ginny. "Please meet Ginny Young."

Luke smiled a thousand-watt grin. "Hi. Luke Watson."

"Hi." Ginny knew she was being rude, but she could hardly look at the man.

Daphne darted a concerned look in her direction before stepping away from Luke and joining Ginny back on the bench. "Ginny might be a new resident here in Payton."

"Yeah? Where you moving from?"

Like she'd ever want him to know anything personal about her. "A couple of counties away."

For a long moment, Luke and Mrs. Reece waited for Ginny to say more. She didn't dare.

"Well, welcome," he said.

When Luke walked off, Daphne Reece narrowed her eyes. "Are you okay?"

Ginny knew she couldn't just shrug. Not if she wanted to finally develop roots in Payton. Not if she wanted to maintain a good relationship with her landlord. "I'm fine. I've just never had much time for cops." Deciding on the spur of the moment to come completely clean, Ginny added, "I grew up in the foster care system. Cops in my life were never a good thing."

As if it was the most natural thing in the world, Daphne Reece took hold of her hand. "Oh, you poor thing. You don't have a family?"

"No."

Daphne Reece teared up and gave her a hug. "Oh, Ginny. I'm so sorry."

As Ginny was engulfed in expensive perfume, she tried to recall the last time another woman had hugged her. It had been a long time. "It's okay. I'm on my own, now."

"Yes, you are. But . . . maybe not for much longer." Smiling sweetly, she added, "If you move in, you'll have me, and I know everyone."

"Well—"

"I'll introduce you to my daughters. They'll

take you to meet their friends. I'm really, really glad you're here." And with that, pulled her into another hug.

Daphne was so warm, so genuine, so loving, Ginny felt her guard slide, little by little. Hesitantly, she patted Mrs. Reece's back. "I'm glad, too, Mrs. Reece. I'm glad I'm moving to Payton."

Chapter Two

Daphne was so excited, she could hardly keep her thoughts straight.

"Jim," she blurted when it looked as if his eyes were about to dart dangerously back to the front page of the paper, "I told Ginny I'd put her under my wing. I'm going to make sure she's settled and happy. I'm going to introduce her to everyone I know. Why, she won't have a thing to worry about here in Payton!"

"Under your wing?" Jim shook his head. "Oh, Daphne. Did the girl honestly think she was about to be adopted when she answered the ad for the apartment?"

Daphne didn't think his attempt at humor was

the least bit funny. "I'm not adopting her, I'm trying to be her friend. Everyone needs friends."

"Maybe she doesn't need any new friends."

"She does." Recalling her skittish behavior around Luke and her mention of foster homes, Daphne sighed. "She needs friends and someone to look out for her."

"I'd say you were trying for more than that. Daphne, give those plans of yours a rest."

Though he'd finally cast the day's *Cincinnati Enquirer* to one side, Daphne had never felt less like celebrating. Once again, her husband thought she was going overboard. She'd heard him say things like 'give it a rest' more times than she could count.

Even after all these years, she didn't appreciate the comment. "Offering my time and friendship was the right thing to do. She needs me."

"She probably does, but I know what *you* want. *You* want to be far more than a friend. You want to be her mother!" Scowling, Jim concluded, "Daphne, the last thing in the world you need is another person to look after."

"If Ginny did want a mother figure—which I'm not trying to be, by the way—it would be fine with me. She doesn't have a mother." Eyes narrowing, she said, "Don't you think that's sad?"

"Of course. But it's not my problem."

Anger bubbled up inside her as she realized just how far apart she and Jim had drifted. Their interests and needs seemed to be on opposite sides of a widening gap—just like that San Andreas Fault in California.

Didn't Jim have any idea that helping other people was what made her happy?

"Daphne, let her be."

Obviously, he didn't.

But Daphne couldn't 'let her be'. She couldn't just take the girl's rent and not care if she was happy or not. It wasn't in her nature.

Jim should know that!

How could a man she'd been married to for thirty-five years be so dense? It was almost like they were strangers. Strangers living in the same house! "Jim, no woman is too old to find comfort in close friendships."

"You sound like a greeting card." Shaking a finger at her, he added, "You're trying to be everything to this new girl: mentor, friend, mother . . . matchmaker."

"The new girl's name is Ginny and I am not matchmaking."

Jim looked at her straight in the eye. "Didn't you say something about Luke?"

She couldn't deny it. "Maybe."

"Daphne."

She was so tired of that condescending tone! "What if I am? Everyone needs a partner in life."

"I agree. But, I think getting involved in Ginny's love life would be a mistake."

"I'm not matchmaking," she said again. "It's not like I planned for them to meet. It just happened."

"It's time for us. What we have now is what we've been dreaming of for years! All five kids are married. They're happy and tending to their own families. It's time to concentrate on us. We're supposed to be kicking up our heels and traveling."

But that was the curse of it all, wasn't it? Daphne realized, looking at her feet. Encased in new turquoise sandals, she knew that she'd certainly had not kicked them up with Jim in months. Gosh, maybe not even years.

They weren't doing much at all, as a matter of fact. She was just about to point that out when she noticed Jim was behind his newspaper once again.

Watching Jim read the paper had become her entertainment. And as far as entertainment went, it was pretty lame. Clearing her throat, she said, "When are we going to do that?"

The paper lowered an inch as piercing blue eyes met hers. "Do what?"

She lifted a foot. "Kick?"

"Oh, Daphne. You know that was just an expression."

"I think we've lost our spark. I think our marriage has gone stagnant. And I'm not too happy about it."

"Stagnant?" Those eyes she knew so well blinked twice. "You really need to find a hobby, Daphne. A hobby that has nothing to do with meddling in other people's lives." After a moment, he brightened. "Like tennis."

Tennis? She did water aerobics three times a week, and that was enough exercise for her. What she needed was Jim.

It was a real shame that he didn't need her in the same way. "If you're not careful, I am going to find a new hobby, and it's not going to be tennis. It's going to be something flirty and fun—and away from you." Just for good measure, she added, "One evening I'm not going to be sitting here beside you watching you read."

He frowned. "I've never asked that you do that."

"What did you expect me to do night after night?"

"Watch TV. Read, too."

Though she'd enjoyed a good book as much as the next person, she'd been hoping for something more. "I may not settle for that. In fact, I may just go kick up my heels with someone else."

Jim slowly put his paper down. "Such as?"

Just to show him she was serious, Daphne stood

up and popped up a heel. "Anyone. Maybe even Hank Wilson."

Jim was so shocked, the paper slid to the floor. "Hank Wilson? We knew Hank in high school!"

"And back in high school, Hank played quarterback. I saw him at the bank the other day. He's still cute."

"He's sixty."

She was almost sixty, too. For some reason, it didn't seem very old anymore. "I bet he kicks up his heels all the time."

Jim's lips twitched. "Well, don't forget we're going to Mary Beth and Cameron's tomorrow. If you plan to go out kicking with Hank, tell him to bring you back at a reasonable time."

Daphne sputtered as she realized he'd deftly called her bluff. No way would she ever go out with another man. But, oh, how she wished Jim would care if she did!

Luke knew there was nothing he could do if a woman wasn't interested in him. Everyone had their own tastes and interests. He was okay with that.

But very few people in his acquaintance actively went out of their way to avoid him.

Which was what Ginny Young was doing. During the past two weeks, he'd seen Ginny five times around Payton. Pumping gas into her old SUV, getting ice cream at the whippy dip, walking along the bike trail. Every time he'd tried to catch her eye, she looked away.

Like she didn't ever want to see him again.

Luke wasn't particularly vain, but her indifference grated on him. He hated that she was traipsing around Payton actively dodging him. Her aloofness, along with the shadow in her eyes when they first met, told him that she was going to be on his mind for quite some time.

Ginny was the type of woman he'd always been attracted to. She was tall. Only an inch or two shorter than his five foot eleven, he knew she'd be the perfect height to kiss. She had long brown hair, with golden highlights. He'd noticed it shone in the sun the other day. Her eyes were hazel and murky enough to get lost in. Well, they would be if she ever looked at him long enough to catch her eye. Every time he'd tried to approach, she'd set off signals that said loud and clear that she wasn't interested in him at all.

He was curious as to why. Was it because he was a cop or because she was already involved with someone? Had she been hurt in the past? Or, did she simply not find him attractive?

Regardless of the reason, Luke knew he wanted to get to know her. He was also tenacious enough to keep trying until she gave him the time of day.

Which is why when he saw her wandering near the Payton Historical Museum, he hopped off his bike and approached. Surely she wouldn't actively evade him in such a benign spot?

"Have you been in the museum yet?" he asked, keeping his voice even and friendly.

Ginny met his eyes, before turning away quickly. "No."

"Most folks say it's better than they imagined—there's quite a bit of history in Payton, especially some interesting stories about Payton's part in the Civil War."

"I'll have to remember that."

"I'm something of an authority on Payton's history," Luke added, acting like he was more interesting than he sounded. Oh, if his sister Pam was nearby, she'd be gagging. Everyone knew he'd never cared much about anything except being a cop.

"Well." Ginny looked like she was trying to look anywhere but at him.

His patience snapped, putting all of his vows to be patient to shame. "Have I done something to offend you that I don't know about?"

Finally those hazel eyes he already knew so well fastened on him. "No."

"So . . . what's going on?"

"I don't know what you're talking about."

Could she sound anymore prissy? He doubted it. "Sure you do," he said. "We've passed each other several times lately, but all you do is look beyond me like I'm invisible."

"That's not true. I've waved."

"Did you move into that apartment?"

After a brief pause, she replied. "I did."

Everyone said it was haunted. The latest occupant, Lindsay Bennett, had even gone so far to admit that living with the ghost had scared her half to death. "Is it going okay?" he asked, being purposely vague. He didn't want worry her unnecessarily.

"Why would you ask?"

Here was Luke's perfect opportunity to describe the history of the place, to come off as calm, cool, and collected. But she was so darn standoffish, he didn't dare. "No reason." Holding up a hand, he pushed away any other efforts on her part. "Look. Sorry I even asked."

For a brief second, she looked shamefaced, but then the expression faded like his dress blues in the dryer. "Well. Good bye."

Luke knew when he wasn't wanted. He was just about to tell her that he hoped she never needed help with a parking ticket when Joanne Sawyer came zipping up along the sidewalk.

He knew Joanne fairly well. Actually, everyone knew Joanne very well. She was Daphne Reece's eldest daughter, married to the town's doctor and ran the historical museum with her sister-in-law Missy.

She also was notoriously accident-prone and walked so fast you'd think her feet were on fire.

"Luke! What's up?" she called out, stopping by his side and clasping his hand in greeting.

Pleased to see that at least someone was happy to see him, he squeezed her hand. "Not too much. Just visiting with one of our town's newest citizens."

Joanne smiled at Ginny before directing her attention back to him. "You're on your bike today?"

"Yep. The weather's been so great I've been biking as much as I can. I usually do bike patrol downtown," he explained to Ginny. "I'm just taking a break."

Ever curious, Joanne turned to Ginny. "Have we met?"

Ginny shook her head. "No. I'm Ginny Young. I recently moved here."

"I'm Joanne Sawyer. Welcome to Payton."

"Thanks."

"Where are you from?"

"Two counties over."

Joanne narrowed her eyes. "Which way? Two counties to the east is all farmland and ranches. To the west is Cincinnati."

"To the east. I grew up in a string of small towns."

"Oh. Are you liking Payton?"

"Very much."

"Do you have a job yet?"

"Yes. I'm working at Make A Mess Preschool."

"The name of that place has always made me smile," Joanne said.

"The kids make me smile," Ginny said. "I'm teaching the four-year-olds."

"I have a new baby. She's seven months."

"Oh. Congratulations!"

Luke could hardly resist shaking his head. Ginny was smiling at Joanne with a genuine grin. Chatting with her like they were long lost soul sisters separated at birth. Joanne, with her usual forthright nature, had gleaned more from Ginny in two minutes of conversation than he had during his last five attempts.

Because neither seemed to particularly care that he was still standing there, he said, "Ginny is living in the apartment above the Sally McGraw Theater. She's renting it from your mom."

"Oh, so *you're* the one. I've heard all about you."

"Really?" That now familiar wariness popped back into her expression.

"Yes, really," Joanne said with a laugh. "If you

knew my mom, you would not be surprised. She's quite taken with you."

"I'm glad."

With a mixture of curiosity and eagerness, Joanne leaned forward. "Have you seen the ghost yet?"

Ginny laughed. "No."

"My mom is fascinated by her. We all are, actually. One night we even had a séance."

Luke chuckled. "You Reeces are too much. Did anything happen?"

"Oh yeah! Music started playing and we all smelled something like powder. The lights flickered, too. The whole thing scared all of us. Even my husband Stratton."

"You'll meet Joanne's family if you're around her long enough," Luke told Ginny. "They know everyone."

"Your mom seems nice," Ginny said. "Very friendly."

Sharing a smile with Luke, Joanne laughed. "That's my mom. She also lives for knowing a lot about everything and everyone around here. If you have a secret, don't tell her!" Glancing at her watch, Joanne stepped away. "Well, if you see the ghost, contact me or Mom or Denise or anyone if you have any problems with her. I don't know if we'll be able to help you, but at least we'll be able to give you moral support."

"Thanks."

When both women turned to Luke curiously, he realized his presence was no longer needed or wanted. "I better get back on patrol. Let me know if you need anything at work or home, Ginny."

"I won't," she said quickly.

Irritation reared its ugly head once more. "You might."

"I doubt it."

Luke was just about to ask her what her problem was when Joanne neatly cut him off. "Have you visited the museum yet?" she asked, clasping Ginny's arm. "Why don't you come on in with me?"

As Luke watched them walk away, he decided to do a little reconnaissance on Ginny Young. There was something about her that didn't make sense. No one could be that aloof and not have something to hide.

When he returned to the station, he did a little bit of checking, he found out that Virginia Young was twenty-six, had an associate's degree in child care, and had grown up since age eight in a series of foster homes. After digging around a little more, he discovered that her parents were killed in a car accident.

Finally he could guess just where her hesitancy toward him was coming from. Police had obviously been involved with her parents' deaths, and authority figures had probably played a role in deciding Ginny's home placement.

For some reason, Ginny's past made Luke feel a little better. At least her disdain toward him wasn't personal. Well, at least he hoped it wasn't.

Chapter Three

Jim Reece wasn't sure what was going on with his wife, but he knew it was nothing good. Every time they were together, Daphne seemed to delight in finding fault with everything he said or did.

And lately, they were together a lot.

Frankly, Jim was getting tired of feeling like he was in trouble. This feeling was new, too. They'd been married a long time, and by all accounts, had enjoyed a very successful marriage.

Together, they'd raised five children. All were married, reasonably happy, and liked their parents well enough to live nearby and be a constant part of their lives.

He and Daphne had been 'empty nesters' for

quite some time. After all, Jeremy, their youngest, had been teaching school for three years now.

They should have been used to living on their own. They should have already adopted new routines, and been comfortable enough to accept each other's foibles. He was.

Well, he'd thought he was. But things had changed. Actually, Daphne had changed, or maybe she'd stayed the same, while everyone else had moved forward. No matter what, Jim was coming to realize that after all their years together, he suddenly had no clue about what his wife wanted him to do.

Hank. Why had she brought up his nemesis from high school?

It was time to have a serious conversation.

After parking his car in the garage, he entered the house, automatically listening for Daphne out of habit. Through the years, his lovely wife had never had a problem amusing herself when she was alone. Either the television was on or she was humming a new song she'd heard while fussing in the kitchen.

More often than not, if her voice didn't lead him to her, her scented candles did. However, this evening, the house was completely, uncharacteristically silent.

"Daphne? You home?"

No answer.

Curious as to where she would be at seven at night, Jim padded into the kitchen, to their ancient chalkboard. For two decades, everyone in the family had used it to tell each other their whereabouts. It was suspiciously blank.

The kitchen counter was, too. No signs of dinner, no familiar appetizing smells. No notes regarding reservations at favorite restaurants.

Actually, the whole place felt as empty as a tomb. Where was she?

Visions of Daphne injured in a car accident made his heart beat erratically. He picked up the phone and dialed her cell phone.

"Yes?"

Her chipper tone made him feel completely relieved . . . and completely irritated. She should be more considerate of his feelings. "Daphne, where are you?"

"At the country club. I decided to meet Denise here for dinner. It's a seafood buffet."

Jim's stomach growled. They'd been going to Payton Country Club for years. A few years ago, the manager had hired a new chef out of Houston, Texas, and had turned the whole dinner menu up a notch. She did amazing things with crab legs.

He picked up his keys, deciding to join her. "Why didn't you leave a note?" he asked, turning off the kitchen light as he headed toward the door. "I didn't know where you were."

"Obviously you found me. What did you need?"

Her snippy tone stopped him in his tracks. "Dinner." As soon as he said it, he wished like anything he could take it back. As "dinner" echoed in the air, even Jim knew he sounded like a Neanderthal. Hastily, he tried to rephrase that. "I meant—"

"You meant that for the first time in recent history, you came home and I wasn't there eagerly waiting for you with dinner in the oven and a warm smile on my lips?"

He winced. "Daphne, that wasn't what I meant. What I meant was—"

"No, I'm pretty sure I know *exactly* what you meant. And don't worry about a thing. I'm sure you'll be able to make a sandwich." Almost grudgingly, she added, "I bought some fresh turkey and ham for you at the market."

Back on went the light. Down went his keys in the little basket where they'd kept keys for years. With some dismay, Jim realized that no seafood buffet was on his agenda for the night. "I see," he said quietly.

"Oh, Jim, don't sound so disappointed. It's not that you even notice what you're eating anymore, between the paper and the news."

Jim looked around his kitchen, at his hand, at his reflection in the mirror. Yep, that was still him. He was still home. Funny, he could have sworn he was in The Twilight Zone.

"You're right," he said, though he didn't think that was right at all. He would definitely notice what he was eating, now that he was going to be sitting home alone on a Friday night.

After a pause, Daphne said, "Well, have a good night. I should be home by breakfast."

Breakfast? Jim almost dropped the phone. "Daphne, what in the world is going on?" His voice drifted off as he realized she was long gone. He stared at the receiver for a moment longer, then softly hung it up. Crossing to the refrigerator, he did, indeed, see two new packets from the deli and a loaf of bread.

It didn't look appetizing at all. Grabbing a soda, he took that and his paper into the living room and sat down. After turning on some music, he sighed. It might be nice to try and read the paper in silence for a change.

But as he skimmed the headlines, Jim had to admit that something was missing. He was used to listening for Daphne's clicking heels as she bustled around the kitchen. Used to hearing her laugh on the phone as she called the kids and checked up on everyone. Used to having her ask him about his day, if he was ever going to put the paper down.

If he was ever going to pay her any mind.

Frowning, Jim knew he missed her. When the phone rang shrilly, interrupting his thoughts, he was glad for the interruption.

"Hello?"

"Dad, what's going on?"

It was Kevin, their eldest, and in many ways, their pride and joy. Kevin had gotten good grades in both high school and college, was extremely successful and had married Missy, who by all accounts was a wonderful, giving woman. Kevin had always been their children's voice of reason, always been honest, always been the responsible Reece.

Unfortunately at the moment, Kevin sounded a little overbearing. A little too judgmental. Jim didn't care for that one bit. "Nothing is going on. What are you talking about?"

"I just talked to Denise, and she said she's sitting at the club with Mom, eating shrimp scampi."

Jim slumped. He loved shrimp scampi. "There's nothing wrong with your mother and sister going out to eat together."

"On a Friday night? You two have always done something together on Friday nights."

Jim nodded in agreement. He'd thought so, too.

"It was time for a change. We're, uh, mixing things up," Jim said, tossing his paper on the floor.

"How come you're not out to eat, too?"

"I wasn't invited."

"What?"

"I guess your mother needed a little time to herself." Thinking to the cold cuts in the refrigerator, Jim said, "Lately, things have gotten all shook up."

"Dad?"

"Don't worry. Your mother's just out for the evening."

"That's not what Denise told Joanne. The girls think Mom is mad at you. What did you do?"

What did he do? "Kevin, why do you simply assume that this is my fault?"

"Because Mom is *Mom*. She's happiest fussing around home. And she's happiest with her routine." After a pause, he added, "Mom likes going out with you on Friday nights. You know that."

Frowning, Jim knew Kevin was right. "She's feeling a little blue, but I think it has more to do with all of you than me," he said, neatly turning the tables. "I think it has something to do with all you kids doing so well, being so independent," he added, saying the last word slowly, and with a bit of contempt. "She's bored."

"I don't understand how that could be. Mom's on more committees than the governor."

"I know that, but she really liked meddling in your lives. You all are so happy now, she doesn't have a thing to do. You know, you really should have made more of an effort to ask her for help and advice." There. How was that for deflecting responsibility?

After a lengthy pause, Kevin spoke. "Dad, why don't you stop by tomorrow morning?"

There had been a distinct note of censure in his son's voice, a note that Jim knew wasn't entirely unwarranted. For the first time, Jim felt as if their roles were being reversed. "You know I have a golf game at seven."

"Come by at eleven. It's important."

Jim was just about to mention that he usually went out to lunch with his friends after golf, but there'd been something in Kevin's voice that made him keep his mouth shut.

Kevin had the same tone Jim had used when they'd talked about finances and his college scholarships. The same tone that he, himself, had used when discussing curfews and the facts of life. It brooked no discussion. Obediently, he said, "All right."

After they hung up, Jim glanced toward the back door, hoping to hear his wife, but instead only heard a crescendo of drums and cymbals as Schubert's *Unfinished Symphony* reached its final movement.

For the first time in a long time, he couldn't care less.

The pizza smelled really, really good. Ginny's mouth watered as she trudged up the next flight of stairs, and tried to be happy her thighs were getting a mini workout as she juggled the pizza box, her tote bag from work, and the day's mail.

She was just about to hunt for her keys when she realized her door was already open. All thoughts of food and relaxation fleeing, Ginny stared at the open door, a chill rushing through her. Hesitantly, she called out, "Hello? Daphne?"

No one answered.

She'd been on her own a long time. Steeling herself, she stepped forward, pushed the door open a little wider. "Hello? Is anyone here?"

She wasn't sure, but she thought she heard a rustle near the kitchen. It was enough to make all thoughts of bravery take flight.

Instinctively, she backed away, turned around, then scampered down the stairs. Finally, she raced out of the bottom foyer and stood on the sidewalk, pizza still in hand. What should she do?

Was it an emergency? Dare she call 911? Every

instinct told her to avoid the cops at all costs, yet her mind was also warning her that fools suffered.

"You working as a delivery man now, too?"

"Luke! Thank goodness."

Glad to see he was in his uniform, she practically hugged him as he sauntered over, his cruiser parked across the street.

"If you're happy to see me, I know something's wrong," he teased.

"When I went upstairs just now, my apartment door was standing wide open. I don't know what to do."

Concern crossed his features. "Did you go in?"

She shook her head. "No, I pushed open the door, but thought I heard something and chickened out. I ran back down, and was just trying to figure out what to do when you showed up."

"Good thing I did. Stay here," he said, already picking up his walkie-talkie looking thing and speaking into it with official sounding acronyms. "I'll go see what's going on. All the way up the stairs?"

"Yep."

Just as he was about to disappear, Ginny called out, "Be careful, okay?"

He flashed her a smile. "Thanks. I will."

After waiting an eternity—though it probably

was only fifteen minutes—Luke stepped outside, his face was grim.

She tried to make a joke. "So, has my imagination gotten the best of me?"

"I don't think so. Your apartment has been robbed. I called for backup. We're going to need to file a report."

She? Robbed? In Payton? "I don't understand."

"Once the other officers arrive, I'll take you up, but it looks like the thieves were out for some quick money. Do you keep cash on hand?"

"Some," she said with a nod, thinking of the neatly labeled envelopes. "I put spending money for the week in an envelope, but I don't think anyone would know about that. As far as everything else, I just have your basic TV and stuff."

Luke nodded but said nothing as he pulled out a notepad and wrote down some notes. A few minutes later, another patrol car pulled up and two other officers joined him. Just being around so many cops made her uneasy. Even the fact that one was a woman didn't reassure her in the slightest. All cops had turned her life upside down on more than one occasion—their efforts to help her had included escorting her to some pretty horrendous foster homes.

As if he sensed her discomfort, Luke cleared his throat instead of touching her arm. "Ready?"

"No . . . but I guess I better be."

He grabbed her heavy tote bag easily, leaving her to clasp her pizza box and follow. The other two officers, after introducing themselves as Officers Crown and Blakely, followed.

Ginny's stomach somersaulted as they climbed the stairs. Now the aroma of the pizza just made her feel nauseated. When Luke opened the door— she noticed he now wore protective gloves— Ginny felt like crying.

Someone had definitely been in her place. With a small moan, she stared at the opened drawers, closet doors, and ripped cords. Her neat little Barbie home was a mess, violated.

Softly, Luke said, "Let's take a tour. Officer Blakely will write down what you think you might be missing, and then we'll dust for fingerprints."

Luckily, both her bathroom and her bed looked untouched. But, someone had pulled out boxes in her closet, and opened almost every single drawer. Clothes and lingerie were scattered everywhere. Her television and stereo were gone.

So was the nifty CD player-alarm clock she'd bought herself last Christmas.

After taking note of those things, Luke touched her shoulder. "Where did you keep your envelopes, Gin?"

No one had called her Gin in years. To hear it

almost made her smile, especially since it sounded almost right coming from Luke. "In the kitchen. Is that bad?"

"It's never your fault that you got robbed, Miss Young," Officer Crown said. "The perps we've caught lately have been robbing for drugs. They're desperate."

Calmly, Luke grasped Ginny's arm. His touch was comforting and reassuring, and warm. To her surprise, Ginny's first reaction was to Luke's masculinity, not the fact that he was a cop.

The knowledge was surprising. Was she beginning to move beyond her past in yet another way? Now, she was forming roots and thinking of police officers as individuals, instead of by stereotypes, and people who were out to hurt her.

Belatedly realizing that Luke was still waiting for her to step forward, she hesitantly smiled. "Sorry, I guess my mind drifted for a moment."

"No problem. Show us where you usually keep your cash."

Sure enough, the two envelopes under her silverware were gone. Ginny winced as the reality of her loss sunk in. "There was a hundred dollars in each envelope," she said.

Officer Crown wrote some notes. "That seems to me like a pretty unusual spot to hide money. Who have you told?"

"No one other than one of the moms at the pre-school." Shocked, Ginny admitted, "She was talking about how hard it was for her to stay on budget—I stupidly told her I'd been keeping myself on track this way for years." As she thought of the single mom, she shook her head. "I'm having a hard time believing she would steal from me."

"We've dusted for fingerprints, we'll soon see. It could be she told a friend, who told another," Officer Blakely said.

At Luke's urging, Ginny sat down. She'd been so sure that she'd been moving forward in the right direction, ready to trust people, ready to plant roots. Now everything she'd gained felt as if it had just fallen through her hands without a moment's notice.

Forty minutes later, the other two officers left, leaving Ginny alone with Luke. Though Ginny was tempted to tell him to leave, she also couldn't deny that she found his nearness comforting.

"I bet you're starving," he said with a smile. "How about I heat up some of that pizza for you?"

"Thanks, but you don't have to."

"It's no problem," he said, going ahead and popping a piece in the microwave.

"Would you like a piece? There's plenty."

"No thanks."

"Luke, I'd be happy to share. Plus, it'd be great to sit with you, if you have time. Do you?"

After a pause, he met her gaze. "If you want me to stay for a while, I have time."

Ginny swallowed hard and wondered if her racing pulse had more to do with the man in her kitchen than any intruder ever could.

Chapter Four

The pizza had been delicious. The company—
to her surprise—had been even better. When
Ginny thought of how different her night would
have been if Luke hadn't offered to stay for dinner
she felt an overwhelming amount of gratitude. She
could only imagine how scared and alone she
would have felt the moment she locked the door
behind him. "Thanks for everything you did for
me tonight," she said after they'd finished off the
last of the pizza.

Luke chuckled. "You're welcome, even though
you've already thanked me. Several times."

Ginny ducked her head as she realized she was,
indeed, sounding like a broken record. Attempting

to explain, she said, "I know I haven't been as friendly to you as I could have been."

"Ginny, you've been downright hostile."

He had a point. "I . . . know. When I think of tonight—how kind you've been—I'm embarrassed. I've done nothing to deserve this," she added, waving a hand toward the coffee table where their plates and glasses now sat empty.

"It's just pizza."

"It's been more than that."

"I won't deny that your aloofness bothered me, but it was your right. You don't have to be friends with everyone in the town, Gin."

"So you stayed here because of your job?"

"No," Luke said after a moment's pause. "Staying here with you this evening had nothing to do with my job."

Ginny caught sight of something in his expression that had nothing to do with police procedures and all to do with the attraction that had stirred under the surface between the two of them. But while he might have been ready to discuss his personal feelings, Ginny wasn't. Not yet. "I'm so glad you were walking by the theater tonight. That was sure lucky."

He blinked, shuttering his emotions once again. "Me, too."

Nervous, Ginny sipped from her soda. Realizing his glass was empty, she hopped up from the couch. "Can I get you another Coke?"

"No, thanks. I should probably get going." He glanced at his watch as he stood up, too. "I was technically off-duty when I saw you on the sidewalk. I need to get some sleep. I'm on again at five a.m. tomorrow."

His words made her rethink their coincidental meeting. "You just happened to be in my neighborhood?"

"Truth?"

"Of course."

Holding her gaze, he murmured, "The truth is I was actually over here to visit you."

Surprise made her glass practically slip from her fingers. Ginny quickly set it down. "Really?"

"Yeah. I was just going to see how you were doing. You've been on my mind."

His words, so sincerely said, made Ginny want be just as frank. "You've been on my mind, too, if you want to know the truth."

"In a good way or bad?"

"Both. I'm not too good with cops."

"Why? You've got a history of crime?"

"No. Foster homes. My head says I'm grown up now, but my first instinct is to be wary of you. Of most people, I guess. This thing between us, it's a problem with me, not you."

"That's good to hear," he said, a slow smile lighting his face.

"Why's that?"

Luke shrugged. "I'm just glad it's not all me."

As Ginny watched him pull on his coat, she didn't know whether she was relieved or disappointed that he wasn't peppering her with questions. She wondered if he knew how hard it had been for her to open up. She suspected he did.

Luke was so different than any other man she'd met. Though he was terribly attractive, it wasn't looks that drew him to her. Instead, it was his character.

Luke was calm. Sure of himself. Straight forward and honest. Those were qualities she admired, traits she wished she possessed in abundance.

She still wished he wasn't a cop.

Interrupting her thoughts, he said, "So, do you feel okay about staying here tonight?"

Though pride recommended she say a definitive yes, the night's activities made her want to be completely truthful. "I'm not sure. When I look around here, all I can think is that just hours ago, someone was here when I wasn't, going through my things."

"That's understandable."

"I just don't have that much." As she scanned her spare apartment, she shook her head. "I don't understand why anyone would steal it."

Compassion filled his eyes. "Why don't you give yourself a break and stay in a motel tonight?"

She couldn't afford that, especially with all her money stolen. She also didn't want to admit how seriously harmed her financial situation was, either. She didn't want there to be anything for Luke to find fault with her about.

Remembering his 5:00 a.m. shift, Ginny walked him to the door. "I'll be fine. I've been in worse situations. Go on home."

Snapping his fingers, he said, "How about I give Lindsay Bennett a call? She's the manager of the theater. Maybe she could come over for a while."

"I've met Lindsay, she's around quite a bit. But, please don't call her. I'll be okay. I have to be, right?"

"Maybe you could stay with Denise Reece? Though her mom helps her out, she owns the place."

The sound of footsteps outside her door prevented Ginny from responding. Staring at the wood, her heart flip-flopped. Had the intruder returned? "Luke," she whispered.

But he had already stepped in front of her. "Shh."

The footsteps shuffled, followed by the shrill clanging of keys. Ginny stepped back.

Luke's whole body seemed to be on edge. Though his pistol wasn't drawn, he looked as if he would be able to draw it without a second's thought.

"Don't move," he whispered when they heard a knock at the door. It sounded forceful and angry. Belligerent.

Who was there?

"Ginny? Ginny, are in you in there? It's Daphne Reece, dear."

Fright warred with confusion, which warred with a relief so intense, Ginny started laughing. Meeting Luke's eyes, she saw he was also having trouble containing his amusement, too.

"Hello?" Daphne called again.

Glancing at the clock, she realized it was close to nine. She was surprised Mrs. Reece was out so late.

"Mrs. Reece, I'm here." Ginny attempted to rush forward, though her legs felt like noodles.

Luke opened the door before she could get to it. "Hey, Daphne," he said. "This is a surprise."

"I'd say you being here is a surprise, too," Daphne said, reaching out to hug him like he'd just returned from the war. "My goodness, I'm so glad you're still here. I was just telling Denise that I was afraid Ginny was here, all by herself." Pulling out of Luke's arms, she turned to Ginny. "Oh, my dear. I've been so worried since I heard the news. Are you doing okay?"

Mrs. Reece was undoubtedly the most warm and giving woman she'd ever met. From the moment she was wrapped in her arms, Ginny no longer felt as if she was all alone in the world. For the first time all evening, she finally felt as if she really was going to be okay.

When they finally pulled away from each other, Ginny looked at the older woman curiously. "How did you know about the robbery?"

"Because this is *Payton*, dear. And, well, I'm *me*. I know practically everyone. Right, Luke?"

Luke shrugged his shoulders. "I know plenty of people Daphne doesn't."

"He does like to tease." Looking from Luke to Ginny, Daphne said, "My, my. Well, as I was saying. Word travels fast, even bad news like yours, Ginny Young. Now, we need to decide what to do about your sleeping arrangements for the evening."

Ginny glanced to the couch and then back to Luke. But before she could say a word, Luke spoke.

"We were just talking about that when you showed up. Now that I know you're here, I think it's time I left." Pausing at the doorway, Luke said, "I'll call you when I find out any information."

As he disappeared through the door, Ginny

forced herself to get a grip. What had she been thinking? Had she already forgotten that Luke had been there as a professional? There was nothing between them, and once more, she knew good and well that there shouldn't be! It would be just too strange to become romantically involved with a cop.

"The minute I heard about the break-in, I rushed right over, Ginny," Daphne said, taking her mind back to the present. "So, you lost all of your spending money?"

"Yes. But how—"

"I have friends in high places." Looking around, Daphne frowned. There were opened drawers and boxes, piles of clothes, and finger print dust everywhere. "Oh, my what a mess. You can't sleep here tonight."

Ginny didn't want to. But she knew she didn't have a choice. Now there was really no money for a motel. And though she had been feeling honest enough with Luke to push aside her pride, she felt it was a completely different thing to tell her landlord that she didn't want to spend the night in her own place. "I'll be fine."

"Yes, you will, because you're going to be coming home with me," Daphne said briskly. "Go pack a bag, dear."

"Are you sure?"

"Positive. I'll call Jim while you're getting ready and ask him to turn down the bed in the guest bedroom."

"That's not really necessary."

"Oh, yes it is. Now, don't argue. It's getting late." Smiling softly, she squeezed Ginny's hand. "It would also make me happy. I wouldn't be able to sleep a wink if I knew you were sleeping here, all alone. It's one thing to know that a ghost is haunting the place. It's quite another to think that a burglar is making himself at home here, too!"

Daphne's warm personality was too hard to resist. "Maybe just for tonight?"

"For as long as you wish, dear."

"Usually I would never take you up on such a thing, but I think I will."

"Never is a long time," Daphne said cryptically. "You'd be surprised to find out the things that happen that you never expected to."

With those words of wisdom ringing in her ears, Ginny opened up the closet door and pulled out her suitcase. Things really were happening that she would have never ever thought would.

As Daphne watched Ginny hurry to her bedroom, she picked up the plates lying on the coffee table and put the pizza box in the refrigerator, after checking to see just how much had been consumed.

Then, she called her husband.

"Where are you now? Out partying down-town?" Jim asked.

She knew his feelings were hurt, and that was why he was so snippy but Daphne wasn't pleased. He should know that she would never go gallivant-ing anywhere. "For your information, I'm at Ginny's apartment above the theater. She was robbed."

As she'd anticipated, his voice changed dramat-ically. "Is she okay?"

"I think so. Just shaken up. Jim, those villains practically ransacked her place. Everything is completely astray! I invited her to stay the night with us."

To her relief, he sounded like the Jim she knew and loved. "Good idea. I'll go make sure the gue-stroom is ready."

"And make a couple of your awesome sand-wiches, too? She may be hungry." In her opinion, a slice of pizza was nothing when there was a cri-sis to contend with.

"Are you?"

Though she'd been at the seafood buffet, noth-ing had tasted very good without Jim's company. "I'm hungry too, dear."

"Good," he said with some relief. "I'll make us all sandwiches."

"And some soup? Would you open a can?"

"Consider it done."

Daphne was still smiling when Ginny came out moments later, holding a black duffle bag and a bemused expression. "Are you sure—?"

"Positive. Grab your purse—let's get out of here."

Daphne was pleased Ginny didn't have to be told twice.

Chapter Five

"Welcome, Ginny," Jim Reece said the moment after Daphne led Ginny in the kitchen, performed a quick set of introductions, and then closed the kitchen door behind them.

"Thank you, Mr. Reece," she replied, liking Daphne's husband right away. He was the perfect complement to the petite Daphne. Where she was all priss and perfection, he was salt and vinegar and good looks. His voice was deep, and deeper lines ran around his eyes, showing the world that he'd laughed a lot and wasn't afraid to let them know it. "It's so kind of you to let me spend the night here."

"It's Jim, and it's no problem at all. Daphne and

57

I are glad to help." Glancing at his wife, Mr. Reece said, "I made three sandwiches, like you asked."

She smiled, almost tentatively. "Thanks, dear." Turning to Ginny, she said, "I know you said you ate pizza, but in my mind, that hardly does a bad night justice. Why don't you sit down, have a sandwich, a glass of milk and I'll pull out the cookies I made this morning." She paused, looking uncertain. "My goodness, I hope you eat cookies?"

Ginny was sure she could count on one hand the amount of times someone had offered homemade cookies right there in their kitchen. "I most definitely eat cookies," she said.

"Then you'll love these. They're snickerdoodles. My son Cameron's wife loves them. She gave me the recipe."

"Sit down, Ginny," Mr. Reece ordered, placing a monster sub sandwich in front of her.

Surprisingly, she did feel hungry and dove into her sandwich with gusto, all in the hopes that she wouldn't seem rude.

In short order, Daphne and Jim joined her after Daphne had placed a large plate of cookies in the middle of the table. "This is very good," she said to Mr. Reece.

He looked pleased. "I'm glad. I used to make sandwiches like this for my boys. Well, for Jeremy. Remember that, Daphne?"

She nodded. "Our youngest was always hungry. I tell you, he could demolish a sub sandwich during a commercial break."

"The other kids guarded their plates whenever he was around," Jim said with a chuckle.

"And he loved cookies!"

Ginny took another large bite in order to hide the grin that was playing at her lips. Daphne and Jim Reece probably didn't realize it, but their life was made up of a thousand references to their children and their likes and dislikes.

She didn't mind, though. It made her feel good to know that there were families like the Reece's. It gave her hope that one day she could have the same thing.

And, Daphne and Jim were just so . . . peppy. They made her laugh. The more she got to know the Reece family, the more she liked them. Each had his or her own quirks, and wasn't afraid to use them. As the couple talked, now having moved to discussing Joanne's newest museum project, Ginny looked around the kitchen.

It was comfortable and cozy. The fabrics were bright and cheerful, the cherry wood cabinets obviously at least ten or twenty years old. But all of it looked loved and casual. Comfortable.

In fact, she'd felt comfortable the moment Jim held out a chair for her and motioned for her to eat. There was something about their home; though it was big, it had a quality to it that seemed to convey a coziness that was sometimes hard to pinpoint.

She took another bite of her sandwich with pleasure, and let herself be led into conversations about the theater, her job at the preschool, and how she wasn't dating anyone.

When each sandwich was consumed, Daphne gathered the plates and set them in the dishwasher. "We'll talk more in the morning, Ginny," Daphne said when they climbed the stairs later that evening. "But please don't worry. I'm a firm believer that everything happens for a reason."

Ginny didn't know if she'd ever had such a positive outlook on things. She certainly hated to think that her childhood had happened for any reason other than plain bad luck. Voicing her skepticism, she said, "Even things like robberies?"

"Even those," Daphne said without a trace of doubt. "I bet one day when we're all very good friends, we'll look back on this night and think there was a reason your house was broken into."

They passed two bedrooms before finally stopping in a suite that had two French doors at the front of it. "Well, here you are," she said with a flourish of her arms.

As the doors opened and a large, lovely room appeared before her, all done in shades of purple and violet, complete with violet covered curtains and a comforter, Ginny knew she had never stayed in such a place. "It's beautiful," she said.

"I like it, too. Jim and I had part of the house remodeled a few years ago. When the kids were little, this was actually two bedrooms." She padded in, looking for a moment like a bell hop in a fancy hotel. "There's your own bath off to the left and a little reading area over by the window seat. In the cabinet are extra blankets and pillows. Hmm. Oh, and in the little refrigerator are bottles of water. But please, dear, go down to the kitchen if you need anything. Don't be shy."

Ginny already did feel shy and overwhelmed. Oh, what she would have given for a room like this when she was growing up! "I can't thank you enough for letting me stay the night."

Daphne treated her to a hug again. "Want to know a secret? I am just as pleased to have you here. Now, get some sleep, and we'll tackle the problems of the world tomorrow. Please don't stay up worrying. It will do you no good! Tomorrow morning will be soon enough. I promise," she finished with a smile.

As Ginny watched her leave, she believed

Daphne Reece was far wiser than most probably gave her credit for.

"The reason we thought you needed to come over here, Dad, is because the three of us have become concerned," Kevin said on Saturday morning.

Jim looked at Kevin, then the solemn expressions on his two younger sons, Jeremy and Cameron. "About what?"

"You and Mom."

"I don't think the time has come that I care to be talked to about my relationship with you and your mother."

Cam exhaled deeply. "We think otherwise."

"Mom's been talking to the girls," Jeremy added.

Jim scratched head. Had there ever been a time when he'd questioned why they'd had so many children? Right at that moment, Jim would have been happy to give four of them away. "What has your mother been saying?"

"You're ignoring her."

He most definitely had not been ignoring her. Why, everything had been just fine the night before, when Ginny came over and he made everyone sandwiches.

But as he glanced at his sons' disgruntled expressions, he figured it was better to say as little as possible. Experience had taught him to let his boys say their piece and then he could do what he wanted.

Cameron leaned forward, resting his elbows on his knees. "Mom's not happy."

So much for keeping his mouth shut. "Cameron, you know how Mom gets. She meddles. She plans. She makes too much out of everything." Thinking back to the other night, he added, "She makes fancy cakes for no apparent reason. She's done this for as long as I can remember. This is no different. She's lonely. I don't think you kids have been spending enough time with her."

"Ha," Cameron said. "I told Joanne you were going to do that."

Jim looked around, half expecting to see more of his precious offspring lurking in the corner. "Do what?"

"Put the blame on us." With a shake of his head, Cameron shook a finger at him. "Mom doesn't want us babysitting her. This sadness is because of you, Dad."

He didn't care for the sound of that. "Now, wait a minute. I may not be perfect, but I love and respect your mother. I've always done my best to make her happy. I still am."

Kevin shook his head. "Not lately."

"I made sandwiches last night."

Cameron rolled his eyes. "Mom needs attention. Your attention." Just like the lawyer he was, he stared hard at Jim. "What are you doing with her at night?"

Jim sputtered. Was his son asking about their sex life? "That's none of your business."

All three boys looked at each other with concern.

Just as if he was on the witness stand, Jim started talking. "We eat dinner together. I read the paper. Your mother putters around the house."

"Maybe you should read the paper a little less, Dad," Jeremy said.

"Maybe your mother needs a new hobby." Though he'd meant that comment to be taken as a joke, the concerned expressions that passed between his sons made his smile falter. "Honestly, boys," And he did mean 'boys', "I think you're overreacting."

"We think you need to give Mom some one-on-one time," Jeremy said, crossing his arms. "Maybe you two could take dance lessons together."

Him, dancing? He'd be the laughing stock of the country club! "I don't think so."

"Biking?" Jeremy asked. "That would be good exercise for both of you. Good for your hearts."

Cameron tossed a pillow at Jeremy. "Mom doesn't bike."

"When was the last time you took Mom out

some place fancy?" Kevin interjected smoothly. "Made her feel special? You know how Mom likes to dress up. Go tell her to buy a new dress. That will make her happy for days."

"Mom loves going to the mall," Jeremy added.

Jim groaned. As if he didn't know that! He'd gotten Daphne's shopping bills for as long as they'd been married. But, it was a small price to pay to make his wife happy—and his sons to leave him alone.

"Take Mom out, Dad."

"First of all—" Jim said, then stopped himself just in time. Maybe the boys had a point. His wife of thirty-five years certainly did like to dine out. As a matter of fact, she loved it.

He couldn't remember the last time the two of them had taken a moonlit walk, either.

Kevin sat down on the ottoman in front of him, just like he used to do so many years ago. "Mom told Denise she misses you."

Jim could no longer ignore his boys' concerns. He'd raised them right, he knew he had. If they were worried about their mother, then they had a perfect right to be. Lord knew that if they were worried that anyone else in the world hadn't been treating Daphne Reece right, he'd be trusting their judgment.

"Long ago, way before we had all of you, your

mother and I used to go driving on Sunday afternoons in the summer. She was real fond of a pink sundress. She wore it almost every week. I thought it made her cheeks glow." Jim closed his eyes briefly, remembering how he'd hold her hand, slip his hand around her waist, kiss her at traffic lights. "We'd look at houses and talk about the one we'd buy one day. Go out for ice cream." Making a decision, he said, "I'm going to reinstate that."

All three boys grinned. "Good idea, Dad."

"That means no family Sunday dinners for one month. You're on your own."

To his dismay, he saw Kevin wink at Cameron. "We'll do our best to get along without you."

"If your mom doesn't like those drives and calls you up, wanting the dinners back, it's not my fault."

"No, sir," Jeremy said, almost cheekily.

"Well, that's settled. We'll go on drives and I'll take your mother out next Saturday night. Now, tell me what's been going on with all of you. Don't skimp."

With a laugh, Kevin handed them each a soda and the four of them talked about kids, wives, stocks, and the Buckeyes, not necessarily in that order. Each asked his opinion about things and Jim did his best to give good advice.

It felt good to be needed once again. That, he could handle.

Chapter Six

"I hope you don't mind me stopping by," Luke said late Monday afternoon.

He'd appeared at Make A Mess just as she was about to dismiss her students. In fact, she'd had them all lined up when he'd appeared at her door, looking as handsome as ever.

"I don't mind at all," Ginny said, realizing with some surprise that she meant it. "I hope you don't mind that I've got my hands full for a few more minutes."

"I don't mind a bit. Hi, kids," he said with a smile as he looked down on the thirteen faces who stared up at him in awe.

The fact that he was so gentle with them made Ginny's heart beat a little faster than normal.

Taking care to put herself between Luke and twenty-six outstretched hands, she said, "School's almost dismissed. The kids will leave this room right at four."

Winking at one of the tiniest preschoolers, Luke nodded. "I'll wait."

Ginny couldn't say why Luke's presence gave her such an adrenaline rush, but it did. It was only through her best efforts that she was able to ignore his presence and help her aides gather coats get the children outfitted to go home.

Of course, the kids loved having a real live police officer in their midst and were showing off for him, making silly jokes and wrestling for places in line.

To Ginny's surprise, Luke only smiled and patiently answered each child's question. The only sign that he had other things on his mind was the way he every so often glanced down at his cell phone.

Finally, right at 4:00, the administrator showed up. It was Mrs. Lance's duty to escort the children to the main room in the building, where their parents would pick them up.

Thirteen hugs later, Ginny motioned Luke into the room and gestured to the lone "big" chair. "Have a seat. I'm just going to wash my hands."

Obediently, he complied.

"You're a natural around these little guys," she said. "I have to admit I wouldn't have thought you would be."

"I have three nephews. They've trained me well."

She laughed, finally settling herself across from him. "So, have you found out anything about the burglary?"

"A couple of things." Slowly, he added, "I was hoping maybe we could talk about the case somewhere else. Somewhere a little more private."

Wariness clicked in. All the trepidation that she'd fought so hard to keep at bay returned in a flash. With some surprise, she realized that she'd mistakenly thought he'd been there to see her for reasons other than business. "Okay. Shall I meet you at the station?"

He laughed. "I was thinking somewhere a little better than that. How about The Grill?"

Now she was really confused. "That's a restaurant."

"I know, Ginny." Leaning his elbows on his knees, he explained. "I want to get to know you better and I thought taking you out to eat would be a good step. What do you say?"

Now she was really confused. Out of habit, she weighed her options. She could insist they have their discussion in her classroom or in the formality of the police station. Both places would necessitate they keep their conversation easy and not too personal. But that's not what her heart was telling her.

Deep down, she knew what she really wanted, and that was to get to know Luke better. "Going to The Grill sounds great."

As Luke watched the play of emotions run across her face, Luke felt his own feelings run the gambit between satisfaction and surprise. When he'd decided to stop by and ask to take her to dinner, he'd done so with more than a little reservation. He wouldn't have been surprised if she had refused to go anywhere with him.

But that hadn't been the case at all. For the first time, Ginny looked relaxed in his presence. And, he was pleased to see, just as aware of the connection between them as he was. "Good. Meet you there?"

She smiled brightly. "Meet you there."

Feeling like he'd accomplished a day's work within a few minutes, Luke strode out of the preschool, then used the few minutes he was in his cruiser to check in with his sergeant. With everything settled, he breathed a sigh of relief.

Though he'd come to see Ginny as part of his official capacity in the case, he was now technically off duty. He'd entered The Grill and had just been seated in a back corner when Ginny entered the restaurant five minutes later.

He couldn't help but appreciate her form as she approached after being directed to him by the hostess. Though he'd seen her at the preschool, he'd been so intent on getting her to go out with him, he hadn't noticed her appearance. Now he took pleasure in it.

Dressed in slim khakis, an oversized denim shirt and brown slip-ons, she looked pretty and understated. Her thick brown hair was pulled back in a ponytail.

She also looked young. He'd mistake her for a co-ed if he didn't know for a fact she was twenty-six.

"Sorry about the wait," she said with a laugh. "On my way out of the building, two kids wanted to show me their finger paintings. I couldn't say no."

That was exactly why he was so attracted to her. Luke loved how she couldn't say no to those four-year-olds. "I didn't mind."

As she sat down across from him, he noticed a slight change in her demeanor. It was more tentative, more reserved than at the preschool. He tried not to dwell on it as they glanced at their menus and finally ordered.

After their server took their menus, Ginny looked at him expectantly. "So, you said you had some news?"

"Some. We got some great fingerprints. They're still getting examined, but right now I think we have a match. It's from a young man who's done some petty thefts around the area over the last six months. He's been picked up before, but never officially charged—we didn't have enough hard evidence. But as soon as we get the okay, we're going to search his house. Maybe at the very least we'll find your envelopes so we can pin him at your place."

"Young man? How old is he?"

Looking at his notebook, Luke said, "Sixteen."

Surprise and a touch of sadness filled her eyes. "I never expected a kid to be my burglar."

Luke shrugged. "It makes sense. A lot of kids have expensive habits. I'll let you know when we find out some more."

"All right."

A frown marred her features and Luke's heart went out to her. "Sorry . . . this was a good lead for us. I forgot from your point of view it seems fairly nebulous."

"Don't apologize; I'm thankful for your work. But," she added with a shrug, "you're right. I was hoping against hope that you'd not only caught my burglar, but had my TV, stereo, and money too."

"Your television and stereo are probably lost

forever. Most robbers pawn those right away. We'll do our best to track their trail, though."

"Okay."

Luke couldn't resist making the conversation more personal. "I hope this experience hasn't soured you on Payton. This kind of thing rarely happens here."

"I realize that. It's why I wanted to live here." After their food came, Ginny added ketchup to her fries, then took a big bite of her cheeseburger. "Payton is far different than every place I've ever lived before."

Luke leaned back, very interested in what she had to say. Maybe she was going to tell him just how nice and attractive the local police officers were? "How so?"

She popped another French fry in her mouth before replying. "Well, all the people I've met have gone out of their way to be friendly. Mr. and Mrs. Reece let me stay in their guestroom last night. That's going above and beyond the simple tenant/landlord relationship, don't you think?"

Though slightly annoyed that she hadn't mentioned him, Luke had to agree. "Jim and Daphne Reece are two of a kind. Actually, their whole family is pretty great. Wait until you start meeting them all—or better yet, get in a place where they're all together!" He shook his head as he recalled his past experiences with a group of Reeces. They could be a loud, noisy group and that was a fact.

Ginny grinned. "Crazy?"

"Controlled chaos."

"Do you come from a family like that, Luke?"

Both the personal question and her use of his first name warmed his heart. He took it as a sign that once again, they were drawing closer. "Not really. I did grow up here, but I only have one sister and one brother. We're close—I see them and their kids fairly often, but the Watson family is nothing like the Reeces."

"Are your parents still here?"

"My dad is. Mom passed away a few years ago."

"I'm sorry."

"Me, too." He took a deep breath. "Looking back, I'd say we were just your average American family. My dad sold insurance, my mom ran us to all our practices. I went to school with Kevin Reece, so I saw a bit of his parents."

He shook his head, surprised at how vivid his memories were. "Even back then, they couldn't ever do anything halfway. One year, Mrs. Reece was in charge of our summer fundraiser and she decided to have a carnival. By the time she was through, our school football field looked like the annex of Barnum and Bailey circus."

Ginny's eyes lit up. "I wish I could have seen it."

"Don't worry. If you stick around, you'll see more than your fair share of crazy things." Quietly, he said, "I guess your childhood was a lot different."

"Like night and day. My parents died in a car accident when I was eight. Suddenly, I was whisked into the foster care system."

"Tough."

"Yeah. It wasn't all bad. The first couple of foster homes were tough, but then I got with a pretty nice family. They kept me all four years of high school and even helped me apply for college and scholarships." Raising a shoulder, she said quietly, "They were good to me, but it wasn't a second family."

She paused to consider. "Actually, it was more like living with some really nice neighbors. I never felt like anything but a guest in their home. I didn't cry when I left . . . and I've heard little from them, other than a card when I graduated college."

"That explains a little about why you've never been especially eager to see me."

"You got it. My head knows that all policemen aren't bad, but my heart remembers sitting in the back of a squad car, wondering who was going to 'have' to take care of me next." Visibly gathering her strength, she admitted, "It's not just policemen, I'm afraid, I have trouble connecting with everyone. I guess I'm still afraid I'll lose them and end up with a mere copy of what I could have had."

"So, how did you get involved in child care? I'm kind of surprised you didn't jump into accounting or computers—something that didn't involve people."

"Computers and math never interested me, but they aren't the real reason I chose being a daycare teacher." Ginny laughed. "Isn't that obvious? I'm still trying to make up for all those years of merely being taken care of."

When the waitress came over to take their plates, Luke picked up the check. "Maybe one day soon we can do this again? Go to the movies or something?"

"I'd like that."

Luke fought hard to control his grin. Finally, he had gained her trust, maybe even something more.

When he walked her to her car, Luke couldn't resist touching her waist to guide her along the sidewalk. He was pleased when she didn't shy away from his touch. "So, are you going to stay back at the theater tonight?"

"I am. Mrs. Reece said I could stay as long as I

wanted, but I'm ready to go home. I went over there on Saturday and Sunday and cleaned everything up."

Though he'd just assured Ginny that she would be fine, he couldn't help but worry about her living in that theater, all alone. "Call me if you need anything."

"I will. I still have your business card. It has your cell phone number on it, right?"

"Right."

Still not ready to say goodbye to her for the night, Luke said, "How about I check things out for you before you head in?"

"I'd hate to impose. But, you wouldn't mind?"

He pretended to think about it. "Not too much."

"All right then, if you don't mind, I'd appreciate it if you came upstairs and looked around. Even when I'm not worried about break-ins, living at the top of an old haunted theater can be a little creepy."

Once again, they drove to the same place in separate cars. Luke waited as Ginny carefully parked and locked her car, then unlocked the outside door for them both.

Luke scanned the area carefully before motioning her into the theater. Everything looked quiet, nothing out of place. "Let me go first," he directed after taking note that nothing downstairs looked disturbed.

Obediently, Ginny followed him upstairs, then stood to one side when he unlocked the door. After thoroughly searching the apartment, he said, "I think you'll be okay tonight."

"Thanks for checking."

"No problem. Don't forget to lock the main door, too." Luke looked at her carefully, wishing Ginny was more open with her feelings, more open to him. "If you want, I could stay while you get settled in for the evening."

She wore a brave smile. "I'll be okay. I promise to lock up every door and window as soon as you leave."

Realizing that was his cue, he stepped back to the stairs. "I guess I'll go ahead and leave. Want to walk me down?"

"Sure," she said with a smile.

As they made their way back down the narrow stairwell, Ginny became aware of his nearness in a way that made everything else in her world fade away. Suddenly, nothing else mattered but the man in front of her, his cologne, his solid presence.

The foreign feelings caught her off guard. Since when did she concentrate on men in her life? Here she was in a haunted theater, with no television in her apartment because of a break-in. But all she could think about was Luke and how nice he was. How well he treated her.

How he truly seemed to care about her feelings and thoughts.

Of course, it didn't hurt that he had beautiful brown eyes . . . and that she'd always been partial to brown eyes.

Their footsteps echoed, until finally they stood next to the door that was her private entrance.

"Well, bye," Luke said.

"Bye—"

She was prevented from saying another word by a sudden popping noise and the ensuing music from a boom box in the main workroom. Every hair in Ginny's body stood on end. Maybe she shouldn't be in such a hurry to tell Luke goodbye?

When she recognized the tune, "Forty Second Street," Ginny relaxed. Well, she relaxed a little bit.

But every muscle in Luke's body had tensed. He laid a reassuring, protective hand on her arm. "Stay here. I'll go check that out."

"Don't. I know what's going on. I'm haunted," she said simply.

His grip lessened, but, Ginny was glad to see . . . didn't leave her arm. "I know I warned you about that, but I didn't really believe there was any truth to the stories. Actually, I kinda thought those stories were just to sell more tickets."

"There might be more to this haunting thing than just stories and propaganda."

As they heard music begin to play, Ginny looked at Luke. "I would go take care of this by myself, but at the moment, I'm thinking that pride is way over-rated. Would you go with me?"

When Luke reached for her hand, she took it in a heartbeat. With a sense of foreboding, they wandered into the workroom, both their eyes glued to the boom box. As if on cue, the music ended, being replaced by static.

The whole episode was eerie.

Ginny shivered, glad she was still grasping Luke's hand.

Luke glared at the boom box like it was a rabid dog. "Why don't we get rid of this thing?"

"Mrs. Reece said not to touch it. I guess Sally's okay, as long as people leave her things alone."

With a flick of his wrist, Luke shut off the knob, then pulled Ginny back to the door. "I'm going to leave and you're going to go straight upstairs."

"Yes, sir."

"And I'm going to call you when I get home and check on you."

"I'll be waiting."

"And I'm going to kiss you because I can't wait another minute," he said, in that same demanding tone.

Ginny didn't have a minute to say a word before his lips touched hers.

It wasn't a passionate kiss. Really, it was hardly more than a quick brush of his lips against hers. But his touch made her feel warm all over. Secure, like someone cared.

Squeezing her hand, he smiled. "This has been fun, Gin. Night."

Ginny was still reliving their night together when Luke called thirty minutes later.

"You okay?"

"I am."

"Any other strange happenings?"

"Nothing. Right now, at this moment . . . I'm just fine."

He chuckled. "Me, too. Good night, Gin."

His words echoed in her mind when she drifted off to sleep.

Chapter Seven

"Girls, do you think my ivory or tan suit?" Daphne said on Saturday night, standing uncertainly in the middle of her beautifully-organized closet. "I'm not quite sure which one your dad has seen me in lately."

Smoothing her hands along her slip, she scanned the rack of clothes again, just like she was hoping something new and special would jump out at her.

Unfortunately, nothing was happening.

Joanne shook her head at both choices. "Neither. Mom, you're going out to dinner, not to a charity function."

Attempting to look at the outfits objectively, Daphne could see how the outfits didn't look especially alluring. Actually, instead of proclaiming romance, they seemed to call out something more along the lines of business professional. But still, she felt compelled to stand up for herself. "These are very nice suits."

"For a grandmother."

They were very classy suits. Expensive, too. But knowing those protestations wouldn't sway her daughters, she stated the obvious. "Girls, I *am* a grandmother!"

"But not Dad's grandmother." With a wink to her sister, Joanne added, "Dad wants to think of you as his sexy wife."

Denise coughed into her hand.

Daphne turned quickly so her eldest daughter wouldn't spy the tell-tale blush that she knew was creeping along her neck. Wouldn't her daughter be shocked if she knew that that had been what she'd been hoping for? "Well, if not a suit, then what? We're going to The Cork." As Daphne glanced again around her closet, she shook her head in despair. Maybe she should forget about wearing anything she had and think about shopping?

Surely there was a sale at one of her favorite stores. She could dash in and buy something attractive and flattering in ten minutes.

Well, in at least an hour. She never had been an especially quick shopper.

"I always liked you in this blue satin dress, Mom," Joanne said, holding out a tea length dress that Daphne had forgotten was hidden in the back of the closet.

Though she'd always loved it, Daphne didn't think it screamed "sexy" either. "Isn't that kind of dressy?"

"Not if you slip on some snappy sandals instead of the matching satin pumps. The midnight color makes your eyes look bright and even bluer, and the cut shows off all those workouts you've been doing at the club."

Daphne flexed her arm and winced. Lifting free weights had been tougher than she imagined. But it would be worth it, if Jim would even notice.

Carrying the dress into her bedroom, she placed it neatly on top of the spread before sitting next to it. "Do you know what happened to your dad, girls? The last time we talked, he acted like I should just amuse myself or bother you kids or play more golf."

She paused, desperately attempting to recall every word of their terrible conversation. "I don't recall a single word about dining out."

As she suspected, Joanne glanced at Denise before turning guiltily toward her. "No, I don't know a thing."

Well, for goodness sakes. Joanne always had

been a terrible liar. Even in third grade when she'd pushed that idiot Joey Arnold into the jungle gym so he'd stop teasing her about her freckles!

Presenting her best know-it-all mother look, she said, "Come now. I know your dad would not invite me out for a fancy dinner for no reason."

Denise slipped the dress off the hanger. "Maybe Dad just decided it would be fun? We all know how he likes a good steak."

"He does, but this sudden desire to go out on the town still seems fishy. Did you put him up to this, Denise?"

"Gosh, no."

"Joanne?"

"Well, I . . . no."

Daphne hoped Joanne's baby Eric would be just as poor of a liar. She deserved some payback. "But you do know, right? Who did? The truth, please."

After deliberating a long moment, Joanne sat down next to her on the bed. "Kevin called a meeting."

That sounded like trouble. "A meeting? What kind of meeting?"

"A boy one." She swallowed hard. "It was necessary, Mom. Dad's been out of control."

"Who attended?"

"Kevin, Cam, and Jeremy."

Denise swallowed as she finally gave in. "Ethan and Stratton came over for moral support."

"When did this happen?"

"A week ago. They talked. Dad realized with all of us on our own and married, he should be spending more time with you."

Obviously the girls hadn't decided to tell the whole truth and nothing but the truth. She snapped her fingers. "And he agreed just like that? I don't think so. I love your father, but this dinner does not sound like his doing."

"It wasn't," Denise said.

Daphne smiled just as Joanne delivered an irritated look her way. "Aha. What happened?" Daphne held up a hand when it looked like Joanne was going to try and be sneaky. "I'd like the whole story now, please. Denise?"

"Kevin made the reservations."

"Kevin?"

"Come on, Mom, you know how Kevin likes to spoil his wife. He's a whiz at romantic dinners. And, for your information, I think he got that trait from you."

The whole truth was hard to swallow. Daphne suddenly felt like a fool, looking for a sexy dress. With a disdainful glare at the blue satin behind her, she announced. "I don't think I want to go out on this date, after all."

"You have to! Cam and Jeremy helped Dad plan the entire evening."

Shocked, Daphne stared at Joanne. "There's more?"

"Oh, yeah. In fact, Missy and Mary Beth should be here any minute to help you with you hair and makeup."

"I've been doing my hair and makeup for a long time. I don't need any help from—"

"You're really going to tell Missy no?" Joanne said in mock horror.

Daphne quickly rethought that. Not only did Missy wear her heart on her sleeve, but Kevin would never forgive anyone who hurt her feelings purposely. "No. I won't say a thing."

"Good," Joanne said. "You have to let her and Mary Beth be involved. They'd be devastated if they thought everyone had planned your night but them."

Heaven forbid. "Of course not," she said, just as the girls walked through the bedroom door.

"Hi, Mom," Missy said with a smile. "Mary Beth and I did knock. When you didn't answer, we let ourselves in."

"You never need to knock. You know that," she said right before she scampered over to Maggie, who was toddling in behind Mary Beth, and Tam nestled in Missy's arms. "Oh, my two favorite girls are here!" she cooed. After cuddling them both, Daphne pulled out the mint green wicker laundry basket she'd set up a few months ago for visits like this.

In no time, she placed a comfy quilt on the carpet, and pulled out several stuffed toys for her granddaughters. Once they were settled, she glanced toward the four older girls in her life.

Daphne smiled at the sight of them all together. Denise and Joanne greeted their sisters-in-law like the best of friends, each of them talking a mile a minute.

Though she and Jim weren't doing the best at the moment, they sure had raised two nice girls. And married their sons off to two wonderful women.

"I brought my ionic straightener," Missy said. "You're going to love it."

Daphne had never heard of such a thing. "Are you sure about that? I usually just put my hair in curlers—"

"Mom. It's time you put your evening in our hands, just like Dad did."

Daphne didn't have the heart to argue any more. As she thought of her original plans to wear a tailored ivory suit and wear her hair the same as always, she realized that she probably did need some changing, just like Jim did. Opening her arms wide, she dramatically said, "I'm ready, girls. Transform me!"

"Oh, brother," Joanne said, right before she and Mary Beth grabbed Daphne's hands and pulled her to the dressing area.

"I never noticed your hair like that before," Jim said later that night, when they were seated across from each other at The Cork.

"That's because I never have worn it this way," Daphne said, thinking how different her hair looked, softly falling in layers around her face instead of curled and teased. Raising a hand to finger a soft strand, she added, "The girls transformed me."

"You never needed much transforming. You've always been beautiful, Daphne. At least you've always been beautiful to me."

"Thank you," she murmured. Fingering the diamond heart pendant that he'd given her when Jeremy had been born, Daphne blinked rapidly, fighting off the appearance of a sudden tear. It was almost irksome to realize just how much Jim's words meant to her, even after all those years. A soft touch or word of praise from him could still make her blush.

Maybe that meant their love was still as strong as ever?

So far dinner had been wonderful. Their shrimp appetizers and Caesar salads had been delicious, and she was looking forward to sampling the grilled salmon. The wine and sparkling water they were drinking were perfect complements. Jim had also been in fine form. So far he hadn't said a thing about work, which was really a first. Usually he shared every minute detail about his cases, just as if she had a vested interest in their outcome.

For her part, Daphne tried not to drone on too much about her various fundraisers. She knew from experience that sometimes Jim thought she put too much effort into her volunteer work.

That left their conversation centering firmly on the kids, which was fine. So far, they'd discussed four out of five and were now planning Jeremy's future.

"Do you think he should be coaching youth soccer?" Jim asked. "Dinah's expecting, you know."

"I know. But, Jeremy loves Bryan. And Bryan needs to keep busy. He's just as crazy as Cameron was at that age." Daphne shook her head, remembering just how wiggly that boy had been. "I think it's a good decision. I told him so, too."

Jim grunted and finished off his coffee. "After dinner, we have two choices. We can go sit in the other room and dance when the band shows up, or we can go . . . home, put on comfortable clothes and watch one of the movies I rented earlier today."

Daphne noticed he fumbled over that word

home; she couldn't say she blamed him. Everything between them was all mixed up and strange. She really did want things back to how they used to be. She'd wanted a little excitement in her life, not the sudden feeling that their home wasn't the place of refuge for the both of them that it had always been.

My goodness, what would she do without him? There was a reason they'd been married for thirty-five years. They were meant to be together.

"So, what will it be, Daphne? Dancing or movies?"

Dancing? Daphne wouldn't have been more surprised if he'd pulled out a lizard and said it was his new pet. Jim Reece did not dance. "Dancing? Where did that come from?"

Red stained his cheeks. "The boys said you might enjoy it."

She would. But she wouldn't if he was going to be miserable. "Oh, Jim."

"I'm trying here, Daphne."

Surprise and gratitude swelled in her. Finally, finally, she was hopeful about their future. Her voice soft, she murmured, "I know that, and I appreciate you trying so hard, too. This has been a wonderful evening."

"I think so, too."

When that all-masculine, self-assured grin that

she knew so well replaced his earlier look of un-
certainty, Daphne smiled back.

Oh, things were going to get back to normal. She
and Jim could start planning nights like this all the
time. Maybe they could join a dinner club! Or, they
could form one—she'd always wanted to do that.

Daphne was just about to say that going home
sounded like a fine idea—that she really would enjoy slipping on her new velour lounge outfit—
when Jim had to go ahead and ruin everything.

"So, does this wing-ding get me off the hook
for our anniversary?"

Suddenly, that chocolate mousse she'd eaten
turned in her stomach. "What?"

He pulled at the snowy white collar of his shirt
as if it was choking him. "We both know there's
only so much of this dating stuff that I can take.
You know I'd rather be sitting at the club."

Sitting at the club. Goodness, for a brief moment she'd almost forgotten that was where he
would rather be. Where he always would rather be.

Playing golf. Playing poker. Watching sports.
Doing any number of activities—all without her!

Anger and hurt coursed through her. "Don't
worry about a thing, Jim, especially not about our
dating future. You're *off the hook* for quite a
while. In fact, I do believe you're going to be *off
the hook* starting tonight. Do not come home."

Jim's self-satisfied smirk evaporated faster than a cup of water in the Sahara. "What in the world brought this on?"

She was so mad, she and her beautiful midnight-blue silk dress stood right up. "I'm not going to do it anymore, Jim. I'm not going to be your doormat, your second-place girl. I'm my own person, and I'm worth a night out every now and again." And because she had a lot of hurt and anger built up—months and months of it, she added, "Obviously we have different needs and interests. I think we need to go investigate them."

"Needs and interests?" Sheer terror formed in Jim's eyes as he stared at her. Good. Daphne didn't even care that everyone was watching them with startled expressions. "Sit down," he said. "You're making a scene."

"I will not sit down. And don't tell me what to do. As a matter of fact, I don't care to ever hear you to order me around again." And with that, she picked up her pretty satin clutch purse, and straightened her shoulders. "I'm leaving."

Her husband looked about to go ballistic. "Not yet. We can't leave until I pay the bill."

"Correction. *You* can't leave until *you* pay the bill for this—this . . . wing-ding. I'm going to go call a taxi."

Frantically, Jim motioned to their waiter, waving his American Express gold card like an S.O.S. flag. After the waiter snatched it away, Jim leaned stood up, too. "Daphne. Calm down. We'll discuss this in private when I take you home."

"You won't be taking me home, because you won't be allowed there."

"Where am I supposed to sleep?"

"How about the club?" she said with not a little bit of vindictive glee. "Or try one of you precious sons. I bet they could come up with plans for that, since you're now relying on them so much."

He narrowed his eyes. "I doubt it. They didn't realize their mother was a spiteful shrew."

Oh! "I'm more than that, Jim Reece. You better look out!" And with that, Daphne scooted back her chair, glared at the Westons two tables over because they were staring, and strode out of The Cork.

It was only when she was standing outside the door, waiting for the valet to go call her a cab, did she realize that she'd be going home—alone—for the first time in thirty-five years.

And because it was dark, and no one was around to see, she let herself cry.

Chapter Eight

"Dad, you should be home right now, not sitting on my couch," Kevin said two days later when he entered the living room.

Jim knew where he should be and he didn't need his eldest son to remind him of it. "Your mother kicked me out, Kevin. Have you already forgotten that you invited me to stay with you for a few days?"

"*One night.* I invited you to stay with us for one night."

Like he didn't realize that. "And I appreciate your hospitality," Jim lied. He did appreciate his son putting him up, but he really missed his comforts of home.

Kevin sat on the arm of the matching love seat,

his expression grim. "I didn't hear that Mom actually kicked you out of the house. I got the impression that it was more like she walked out on you at the restaurant."

No matter what happened, it hadn't been pretty. "Same difference. I was left sitting there like day-old bread. Everyone's been talking about it. I've been humiliated. Until she apologizes, I'm not going home."

Kevin sighed. "Dad, you're not being reasonable."

"I know how I'm being, son." Stubborn, pig-headed. Difficult. Jim also knew that he couldn't seem to help himself. The stress of the situation was putting every one of his faults on parade. Just to divvy out the misery, Jim glared at his eldest son. "I personally feel that this whole terrible situation is your fault."

"My fault?" Kevin's voice rose. "I had nothing to do with any of this."

From the corner of his eye, Jim saw Kevin look toward Missy, who'd just come in. Their shared glances made Jim feel like he was two-years-old. He didn't care for the feeling. "You and your brothers are the ones who insisted I take your mother out to that fancy restaurant. If we'd never gone, I'd be home right now, sitting in my own chair."

Jim patted the seat twice for good measure, eager to completely switch the focus of their conversation. "And speaking of chairs . . . Kevin, this is just about the most uncomfortable couch I've ever sat in. Why you enjoy this modern nonsense, I'll never know."

"The couch is fine, Dad."

"It might look good in a fancy magazine, but it's tough on my back. How much did you pay for it?"

"I don't know."

"I bet it was too much. Someone really took you for a ride. Maybe you can get a refund?"

To Jim's shame, Missy looked mortified. "Oh, gosh, I'm sorry Dad. Maybe if I got you a pillow—"

"He's fine, Miss," Kevin said. Jim couldn't help notice that even though Kevin was having no trouble glaring at him, his tone to Missy was gentle and sweet. Like she was precious.

Daphne and he had often hid grins at the way their son treated his wife. They never said anything aloud, though, knowing that Kevin's chivalrous treatment was because Missy's first marriage had been abusive.

But Kevin had no gentle tones for his father. "You need to settle down. It's not my fault the dinner didn't work out. Dad, you messed up."

"Didn't work out? Kevin, the whole thing blew up in smoke! She yelled at me in front of a crowded dining room, left me in the middle of the restaurant, took a taxi home, and even said I wasn't welcome in my own house. I'd say it couldn't have been any worse."

Kevin glanced at Missy once again. She was holding Tam, their daughter and looking at Kevin like he was the only man in the room who was capable of reason.

"I think I'll go check on dinner." Almost apologetically, she said, "We're having fish sticks and macaroni and cheese. I hope that's okay."

Jim inwardly groaned. He'd sworn off fish sticks when their youngest had turned eight. "That sounds great, dear."

After she left, Jim turned to Kevin. "Call your mother. I want to know what she's doing while I'm cooling my heels here."

Kevin visibly fought to control his temper. "All right." He picked up the receiver, but paused before pushing any buttons. "Are you going to behave while I talk to her?"

"I won't say a word."

"You better not." With precise movements, Kevin picked up the phone and dialed quickly. "Hello, Denise? Hey. Where's Mom? Oh. Is she okay?"

As Kevin rested against the wall and rubbed his head, Jim stood up. "What's going on? What's wrong with your mom? Does she have a migraine? Is she injured?"

"Hush, Dad." Turning away, Kevin talked to Denise once more. "Nothing. Dad's still here." Looking at Jim, he said, "He's going to stay here another night, I guess. What? Really? Wow. Hmm."

Really? Wow? Hmm? Something sounded wrong. Jim wished Kevin would face him again so he could get the scoop.

"I didn't know that. Well, all right. Yeah, we'll be here."

After another long minute, Kevin hung up.

Jim stood. "What's going on? Is your mother sick? Crying?"

Wearily, Kevin said, "It seems Mom still doesn't want you home for a while. Cam's on his way over there now to get some more of your things. He'll bring them by later."

With dawning appreciation, Jim realized he had to face the truth. This was more than a spur of the moment fight. Things between Daphne and him were not going well. In fact, they were pretty much on a road to disaster. "Things are worse than I thought," he murmured. "I wonder if your mother is ever going to want me back."

Kevin sat down next to him. "She will. She loves you."

"It doesn't sound like it." After a pause, he said, "It doesn't feel that way, either."

When Missy came back in, she joined them. "What happened that made you and Mom so upset with each other?" she asked. "I've always thought you two were really happy."

"I thought so too, until the last couple of weeks."

"Did she even like the dinner?" Kevin asked.

"She loved it," Jim said. "Everything went like clockwork until I said the wrong thing."

Kevin and Missy shared a look again.

"What did you say?" Missy asked.

Jim swallowed hard. "I, uh, said I was glad I wouldn't have to wine and dine her anytime soon. That's when your mother got all bent out of shape."

Missy winced. "Uh oh."

"Actually, I think I said something like, 'I'm glad I'm off the hook now.' She didn't care for that expression."

"Dad, you were supposed to say nice things to Mom," Kevin said.

"I don't need you boys telling me how to treat your mother."

"You obviously need some help, because so far you're doing a pretty horrible job."

Only lately. "She's just bored."

"I don't think so."

"She is. She wanders around the house, making cakes and casseroles neither of us wants." He shook his head. "You should have seen how excited she was when that Ginny Young came over the other evening. She was like her old self, bustling and helping."

"Then you need to entertain her."

Jim fought off a smile. He was proud of his sons, proud of how they loved their mother and wanted the whole world to do everything for her.

He agreed. But he also knew in his heart that he wasn't her only problem. His wife was going through her own kind of mid-life crisis, and he was at a loss of how to help her deal with it. Somehow he knew buying her a snazzy red convertible or taking out on the town wasn't going to solve all her problems.

"I don't know how to make her happy right now, Kevin," he admitted, completely serious. "I don't know how to make her happy without completely redoing our lives, and for the life of me, I don't think that's the answer. She needs time to decide what to do, so I guess that's what I'll give her."

"You really love her a lot, don't you Dad?" Kevin said.

"More than you know." With a sigh, he said, "I hope you two never go through this."

Missy kissed Kevin's cheek. "I hope not, too." When Tam toddled closer, Missy glanced at Jim. "Would you mind watching Tam while I finish dinner?"

Jim held out his arms. When Tam went to him, he scooped her up and cuddled her close. "Take your time, Missy. I love holding Tam."

She winked. "I was hoping you would say that."

"Mom, don't you think you're being kind of mean to Dad?" Joanne asked.

Daphne figured she probably was. But at the moment, she didn't care. "I've given that man the best years of my life. All I'm getting in return is a lot of nothing."

Out of the corner of her eye, Daphne spied Joanne roll her eyes at Denise. Oh, their complacent attitudes were driving her mad. They had no idea what she was going through.

Thank goodness.

Feeling bad for burdening them all, she attempted to smile. "Don't worry about a thing, girls. Everything's going to be just fine. Why don't you just go on home? I'll be perfectly fine sitting here by myself."

"We're not leaving you alone like this, Mom," Denise said. "How about some hot tea?"

"That sounds heavenly."

Hastily, Denise started a kettle to boil, leaving Daphne alone with Joanne. Her forthright daughter. She usually was proud of Joanne's qualities. But for now, they just made her want to run and hide from those piercing eyes. "Jo, there is not a thing you need to be telling me."

"Really? That's strange. I thought you believed in helping other people."

"I do—when I'm the helper. I don't care to be on the receiving end and I'm not very good at accepting advice. Especially from my children."

"Children." Joanne laughed. "Mom, I'm almost thirty years old."

"You'll always be my little girl."

"Oh brother."

Daphne held her tongue, wisely knowing that years from now, her daughter would say she was right. No matter how old Joanne was, Daphne would still remember her with long red hair and skinned knees from chasing after her brothers.

"In any case, there's nothing you can do for me now. I think your dad and I just need a break from each other."

"Break? You two have been married too long to take breaks! You need to be living together, under the same roof. Working out your problems."

"I don't happen to agree."

When Denise walked in, she sat next to Joanne,

making what Daphne supposed was some kind of united front. She steeled herself for the next on-slaught. The next unasked-for onslaught.

Joanne didn't make her wait long at all. "Dad's sitting in Kevin's house grousing about his furniture!"

"What?"

"Kevin just called," Denise said. "I guess Kevin was just told that he needed a new couch."

"Really? Which one? I always thought his furniture was very comfortable."

"Mom!" Joanne really looked as if she was going to come unglued. "You and I both know that if Dad said a word about the furniture that Missy probably feels horrible and that Kevin's about to strangle Dad for making her upset. Dad should not be over there."

"You may be right about that, but I don't want him home. Not yet."

Denise popped up again, returning two minutes later with a tray of tea. After handing Daphne a cup, she seated herself across from Daphne gracefully.

"It's been two days and nights," she said. "What are you hoping to accomplish, Mom? Dad's sleeping over at Kevin's, Cameron's on his way over here to sort through more of Dad's clothes, and the rest of the family is in an uproar, too. I don't understand how it all happened."

In her usual blunt style, Joanne said, "What we want to know is . . . why aren't you happy?"

"Things between your dad and me have gotten stale. We've started living separate lives." After taking a fortifying sip of steaming tea, Daphne added, "Girls, I don't want to divorce your father; I just want him to want to be with me."

"Dad does," Denise said.

"Not lately."

Joanne bit her lip. "Maybe you two should get counseling."

"We are too old for marriage counseling. Once more, we don't need it. Why, we could counsel people on their marriages."

"Obviously not." After sharing a glance at Denise, Joanne said slowly, "Maybe you need a job, Mom."

Daphne felt as if she'd just been slapped. Betrayed. How many times had Jim blamed his lack of attention on her lack of outside interests? Now her children were telling her the same thing?

"I don't need to be busier. I just don't want your father to take me for granted." Daphne felt her cheeks heat as she realized she'd practically screamed the last bit. But, she couldn't help it. "I want him to be happy with me when he comes home."

"He is, Mom. You know you make him happy."

"I suppose."

The doorbell's chime couldn't have come at a better time. Eager to get a break from her pushy daughters, Daphne hopped up. "I'll get that. I guess Cam's already here."

But it wasn't Cam. It was Ginny Young, looking apprehensive and terribly shy. "Mrs. Reece, I'm sorry to drop by unannounced, but I was hoping you might have a moment to talk?"

All of Daphne's problems fell by the wayside as she took in Ginny's worried expression. "Ginny! How nice to see you. Come on in, dear. Girls, look who dropped by."

When Ginny spied Joanne and Denise, she colored bright enough to practically glow. "Oh, I'm so sorry! I didn't realize you had company." Shrugging back on her jacket, she backed away. "I'll come back later. I mean, I'll call you later—"

"These girls aren't company; they're my daughters. Remember Joanne and Denise?"

"Hi. I'm sorry I barged in like this."

"We're glad you're here," Denise said, striding forward. "Come on in."

"Yeah, it's just us," Joanne said with a sarcastic look at her mom.

But as she turned to Ginny, Daphne noticed that Jo's expression softened. "Ginny, believe me, we're happy to see you. Come sit down and join us."

Denise retrieved the tea set and brought out another cup. While she was doing that, Daphne asked questions about Ginny's cute scarf, exclaiming in admiration when she found out Ginny had knitted it herself.

Finally, when all the pleasantries were over, Daphne looked at Ginny more critically. Underneath the cute pink scarf was a rumpled shirt. She looked tired and more than a little bit confused. "Ginny, what's wrong?"

Denise frowned. "Please don't say you've had another break-in!"

"No, nothing like that, though Luke did say that he had a lead." After sitting down, she said, "Mrs. Reece, I'm wondering if maybe moving to Payton was a big mistake."

Daphne was flabbergasted. "Really?"

Ginny was tempted to grin when all three Reece women gasped in surprise. Though she was hurting inside, she'd observed enough people to enjoy the way the three women acted like a complete unit. And how fiercely loyal they were to their little town.

Ginny admired their loyalty, though she had to admit it was hard to fathom.

Daphne started talking like she was on fast-forward. "Have people been mean to you? Is it your job?"

"Is it the apartment?" Denise asked. "Don't feel bad if it is; a lot of people aren't real fond of living with ghosts."

"No, the apartment's fine." She corrected herself, hoping to be as honest as possible. "Actually, living above the place is kind of crazy, what with the play rehearsals going on and Sally lurking around at night."

"And the break-in," Joanne added cryptically.

"I'd be lying if I said the break-in hadn't spooked me, too," Ginny admitted, feeling even more embarrassed for stopping by unannounced. Obviously, the three women had been having a serious conversation. All of them looked tense and on-edge. Ready for a fight.

"So what is it?"

"I—" Ginny felt her face heat. "It's—"

"Your job?"

"No. I like it fine." Thinking of her little students, so eager to learn and be with her, Ginny's voice softened. "I really like my job."

"Then what is it?" Daphne asked, looking completely puzzled.

"I think I know." Joanne flexed her fingers. "If it's not the town itself, it's not work, and it's not the place—though no one would fault you if it was—it's gotta be man trouble."

Denise folder her hands across her chest. "Honestly, Joanne. Not every woman dating in this day and age has problems . . ." Her voice drifted off as Ginny realized her expression said it all.

Daphne clapped her hands. "It *is* man trouble!" Leaning forward, she peered at Ginny like an optometrist. "Who's troubling you?"

Luke wasn't *troubling* her. It was more that he was disturbing her, right? Ruining her sleep? Making her rethink her future? "Luke."

"Ah," said Daphne.

"I knew it," said Joanne.

"Luke who?" Denise asked.

"Officer Luke Watson," Daphne said, smiling broadly. "Luke's family has lived in Payton for decades. Kevin went to school with him. Luke is almost six feet tall and has the most gorgeous jaw of any man I've ever seen. He's just dreamy. I introduced Ginny and Luke to each other."

"Oh boy," Denise said.

Joanne leaned against the couch with a sigh. "With everything going on, I'd forgotten all about that." Turning to Ginny, she said, "Ginny, my mom has a horrible habit of match-making and getting into other people's business. Please don't feel bad if you have to tell her to stay out of your life."

With a shrug, Denise added, "Mom means well."

Pointedly ignoring her daughter, Daphne said, "So, do you like him, Ginny? The moment I saw the two of you together, I was sure there had to be something very special between the two of you."

Daphne's words sounded like she and Luke were planning a trip to the altar! "I'm not sure. I mean, we're still getting to know each other."

"If she's not sure, that means he's been on her mind," Joanne said sagely. "I never knew what to think of Stratton when we were dating. Well, actually I did," she corrected herself. "It was more like I didn't know what he thought about me."

"I know what Luke thinks about me. At least, I used to. He thinks I'm skittish and too distant. He might be right. We're complete opposites."

"I've never found you to be like that. I thought you were very sweet from the moment I met you. And I'm never wrong." Daphne said loyally.

"You might be this time. You haven't seen us together."

"Now that I think about it, I have to admit you did seem awfully cool to Luke when I saw you both outside the museum. But that was almost two weeks ago."

"I was rude," Ginny corrected. "Thankfully, I've behaved better since then."

"Don't worry. Luke Watson really is a nice guy."

"I know. And the way he kisses—" Mortified, Ginny popped her right hand over her mouth.

"He's kissed you?"

"Yes."

"Aha," Joanne said.

"How was it?" Daphne asked, like she was truly curious. Like Ginny would have no problem sharing all the details with her and her daughters.

When all three leaned forward, she said, "Good."

"I thought he would be. Oh, those shoulders."

"Mom!" Denise said, shocked.

"I merely thought about it, dear. I haven't kissed him."

Ginny did her best to interject. "As I was saying, I'm sure Luke is a great guy . . . I just don't know if he's for me. We might be too different."

"Well, getting back to opposites, I have to admit that Jim and I were opposites at one time, too. Now, why, we're just two—" Daphne covered her mouth with her hands. "Oh my goodness! I can't believe I was about to say we were so close!"

"Aha!" Joanne said, her voice filled with glee. "You do love Dad."

"Of course I love him. I just—"

Ginny couldn't resist joining the gentle teasing. "It's just that he's driving you crazy?"

"Absolutely," Daphne said, wonder in her voice.

"Looks like you both have it bad," Joanne laughed.

"Oh my goodness," Daphne said, staring at Ginny in surprise. "I do believe she's right!"

Chapter Nine

"Think we're making progress, Jake?" Luke said to his sometime partner on Wednesday afternoon.

"Some. I heard you made an arrest in the theater robbery."

"Well, I brought the kid in. We haven't officially pressed charges yet. At the moment we're holding him for questioning and attempting to locate his parents."

"Attempting? I thought he was only sixteen. Doesn't he live at home?"

Recalling the background of the boy, Luke clarified. "I think *he* lived there. I'm not sure his parents did."

"Broken home, huh? I'd be surprised to find any-one married for longer than two years these days."

"No, his parents are married."

"Where are they living, then?" Crown men-tioned a low-income apartment complex. "There?"

"Not at all. It's just the opposite. This kid is ac-tually from a wealthy family. They live over by the country club. They're members."

Jake scratched his head. "And the kid steals be-cause . . . ?"

"It's guesswork right now, but I'd say it was for attention. Both parents have kind of high-profile jobs, both work for major companies and travel constantly. I guess he wanted them around a little more."

"I have a feeling he's going to get his wish."

"And more than he dreamed of," Luke added. "No matter what his reasons, he's made quite a few bad decisions. When he heard from a pal who has a little sister at Make A Mess Preschool about Ginny's saving system, things went downhill fast."

Crown tapped the report. "On the bright side, sixteen is young enough to avoid a permanent record. Hopefully he'll be scared enough to use this whole experience as a learning one."

"I hope his parents take it as a warning for them, too. We've seen enough to know that nothing takes the place of old-fashioned supervision." As he looked at the paper one more time, Luke shrugged. "Of course, the boy's future lies in Ginny's hands. It will be up to her, the boy's lawyer, and the department to decide what to do next."

"What do you think Ginny is going to want to do?"

"I couldn't make a guess. Ginny knows a lot about difficult childhoods, but she also works hard for her money."

"How serious are the two of you getting?"

"We're just dating a little. We had pizza together. Grabbed a quick bite at The Grill." And they'd kissed. Held hands.

He'd wanted to do more.

"And . . . ?" Jake pressed, pretty much reading his mind.

Luke had known Jake Crown way too long to lie. "And . . . I'd like to see her more. There's something about this girl that makes me smile. Ginny Young looks like she's all sweetness and light, but then she's got this tough attitude that makes me second guess every word I say to her."

Thinking about the crazy combination of emotions he'd felt while eating dinner with her, Luke added, "She makes me uneasy and feel ten feet tall all at the same time."

Jake cracked up. "When you get it, you get it bad! You're crazy about this girl."

"Or just plain crazy," Luke admitted with a grin.

"So, when are you going to see her again?"

Luke glanced at his watch. "In a couple of hours. After the boy's parents are contacted, I'm sure we'll need to speak with Ginny."

"That will be tough, directing the questioning with her in there."

"I'm going to be in the room, but I asked not to be a part of the discussion. Ginny can be so skittish, I don't want a thing like this to come between us."

"Assuming she feels that there *is* something between you two."

"She does," Jake said confidently, wishing he felt as convinced inside as he sounded.

There was still a part of him that wondered if he was the only one thinking about a future together.

"So, Miss Young, given all that you have heard, what would you like to do?" Lieutenant Carrington asked.

Ginny shifted uncomfortably in the hard wooden chair across from Lieutenant Carrington, two police officers, and the boy's lawyer. Also in the room, but standing over to the side, was Luke. So far he hadn't said a word, only winked when she entered the room.

When the lieutenant had called her, he asked if

she'd be willing to sit in a conference room and discuss things instead of proceeding more formally. Eager to put the whole experience behind her, she'd readily agreed.

Focusing on the question, Ginny folded her hands on the table so no one would see how nerve-wracking the whole experience was for her. "I'm not quite sure about what to say," she admitted. "On one hand, I really do feel for James. But, on the other hand, he broke into my apartment and stole my money."

Mr. McCoy, the boy's lawyer, spoke next. "James' parents want to assure you that they want to reimburse you for the loss of you television, stereo, and cash, along with compensation for your troubles." He paused, glancing at the lieutenant as he did so. "We know you spent several nights away from your apartment and had to get your locks changed."

"I would appreciate that."

Mr. McCoy nodded and wrote down some notes.

The lieutenant looked at Ginny, his expression gentle. "You're the victim here, Miss Young. Do you have any other concerns that need to be addressed?"

Summoning up her courage, Ginny nodded. "I guess it's probably written in my file somewhere, but for the record today, I'd like to share that I was a foster child. My parents died when I was young and I had nobody to step in for me. I went through some difficult times."

She took a deep breath before continuing. "So, while I feel for the boy and his circumstances, I have to admit that I don't feel sorry for him. The money that he took was probably nothing more than pocket change for him. To me, it was living expenses for two weeks."

Mr. McCoy looked uncomfortable, but both Lieutenant Carrington and Luke nodded their encouragement. "That said, I'll go ahead and drop the charges and accept the monetary compensation. But, I also want a note of apology from James and his parents."

Mr. McCoy stopped writing and chuckled. "You sound like a teacher."

Her chin lifted. "I am a teacher. But I'm more than that, too. I think I have a right to be apologized to."

She sneaked a peek at Luke to see how he was reacting to her little speech. Catching her eye, he nodded slightly.

Feeling like she had his support, she continued. "I just want this boy to know that his prank had consequences, not just for him . . . but for other people."

"Consider it done," Mr. McCoy said.

Lieutenant Carrington eyed her with new respect.

And when Ginny glanced again toward Luke, she felt as if she finally had someone in the world on her side.

Luke Watson was smiling broadly.

"This will conclude our meeting," Carrington announced, standing up. "McCoy, please speak with your clients and let us know how you wish to proceed."

"Will do." After shaking Ginny's hand, he walked quietly out.

Ginny had just breathed a sigh of relief when Lieutenant Carrington held his own hand out to her. "Well-said, Miss Young. Thanks so much for saying what you did."

"You're welcome."

Luke walked to her side. "I'll walk you to your car," he offered, the moment they were back into the crowded halls of the police station.

Ginny felt so emotionally drained. All she wanted to do was sit in a hot bath. "I'll be okay. Walking me out's not necessary."

"Maybe not for you. For me, it is."

Cradling her elbow, he escorted her through the rest of the building. As they walked, more than a few interested heads turned their way. A few officers grinned at Luke, but no one was disrespectful.

Finally, they walked out into the waning sunshine. "Oh, it feels good to be out of that place," she said. "I'm sorry, but police stations give me the creeps."

"You did good in there, Gin."

"Do you really think so? I probably shouldn't have said anything."

"It was your right. I'm glad you did."

Luke smiled as his hand moved from her elbow to the small of her back, sending little pulse points of awareness through her. Together they walked down a series of cement stairs, across a patch of pavement under construction, and finally around a haphazardly planted bed of flowers.

Gesturing to the somewhat lopsided pansies, Luke said, "We were the third grade's town beautification project."

"The flowers look good here," she teased. "They really spruce up the parking lot."

Luke laughed. Ginny felt suddenly brighter inside, like everything was going to be okay. The emotion was a good one, especially after the tumultuous feelings that had been exploding within her in the courtroom.

"What do you think is going to happen now?"

"I think you're going to get your money back with interest and some carefully worded apology notes."

"I hope so."

"Just for the record, I think you're pretty incredible, Ginny Young. You make me smile."

Her feelings toward him were way more complicated than that. She felt drawn and scared of him all at the same time. "You aren't so bad, yourself," she said, wincing at how lame her words sounded.

"I'll take that," he quipped. As they reached her car, he tapped the hood. "Any chance you'll let me take you out to dinner to celebrate?"

There was a very good chance. Everything that had happened lately made Ginny realize she no longer wanted to merely live on the sidelines and hope for the best. She wanted friends and love and a future even if no one could guarantee that things wouldn't be perfect forever.

She knew part of this realization came from her contact with the Reece family. Their relationships with each other were special and it was evident they all respected and cared about each other . . . even when they were meddling and spouting opinions.

In short, they all knew they were loved.

She wanted that.

Instead of just merely observing, she wanted to grab life with both hands and do everything in her power to hold on tight.

Half teasing, she said, "Why do you want to take me out? Is it an officer/citizen thing?"

"Nope." Leaning close, he said, "It has nothing to do with my job or your robbery. As a matter of fact, I think you need to take criminal activity completely out of the equation."

His scent brought back memories of their kiss in the stairwell. Leaning closer, she murmured, "So, it's more of a man/woman thing?"

"Definitely. What do you say?"

"I say yes."

"Great." Looking pleased, Luke said, "I have Saturday night off. How about I pick you up at seven? We could go to the Payton Country Club."

Country clubs were completely foreign to her. "Is it dressy?"

"Nope. Well, not really. No jeans, but anything else will do."

"All right. I'll be ready at seven."

"I'll see you then," he said, squeezing her shoulder. Before she could reply, he kissed her again, pulling her gently into his arms and making the rest of the world seem unimportant.

And right then, at that moment, Ginny was pretty sure she could get used to life with Luke.

Chapter Ten

Two more days had passed. Jim was getting pretty tired of living out of a suitcase. He was even more tired of being bossed around by his sons.

"Dad, I think you need to come over with me to Mom's flower show," Jeremy announced the moment he arrived home from his job teaching high school history.

He knew he 'should', but at the moment, he'd rather eat nails. "I don't think so."

As Jeremy took a deep breath and figured out what to say to that, Jim shuffled his paper and tried to get settled on Jeremy's living room sofa, but it was a useless endeavor. The couch was riddled with lumps and had next to no back support.

Honestly, did any of his kids believe in comfortable furniture?

Kevin's place was filled with slick, contemporary stuff that all looked like it would fall apart if a guy his size sneezed too hard. Jeremy's furniture was just plain old.

"Dad—"

Jim neatly cut him off. "I've been to a dozen of these shows, Jeremy. I could probably run a flower show if I had to. I don't need to go to this one."

"But Dad—"

"If you think it's important, go without me."

"I think you're forgetting the point. Mom would be really happy if you showed some interest in her work. She's been working all day to set it up."

"She always works all day to set it up." Jim shifted again, wincing as an old spring greeted the middle of his lower back. If he ever found the perfect spot, he wasn't going to move an inch.

Folding his arms over his chest, Jeremy looked the same way he did when he was six and wanted the tooth fairy to come during dinner. "You could just go for a little while," he said. "Fifteen minutes. Then you could tell Mom you came to see what she's been working on."

For a moment, Jim considered doing just that. Lord knew he'd visited her shows dozens of times before.

But then he thought about what would happen and he shook his head. "Jeremy, if I stopped by, your mom would wonder why I was there. Then, I'd call something a daisy and she'd spout off the Latin name for it and I'd feel like a fool. Finally, I'd try to smell one of her fancy plants, just to be informed that those flowers aren't supposed to smell good."

"This time might be different."

"It won't be." Jim groaned as he attempted in vain to prop his feet up on the too-dainty ottoman. "Besides, your mom wouldn't notice if I was there or not."

"She would, Dad."

"Doubt it."

"Mom planned—"

Jim cut him off. "For hours. I know. She plans everything for hours. She makes a big deal about everything."

Except him lately, Jim wanted to add but didn't. It wouldn't do for his kids to realize just how lost he'd felt without his wife. Over the years, he'd come to depend on her for everything: from washing his socks to giving him an encouraging smile when a case was going poorly to helping him remember to control his cholesterol.

Jim knew he was a mess without her.

He'd tried to be there for her, too, but perhaps

he'd failed. Maybe he should have listened to her more closely, tried to help her more often. Wined and dined her with more finesse. Monitor her cholesterol?

But over the years, they'd been so busy raising kids, then paying for their education, then doing everything in their power to get them happily married and settled, there just hadn't been a lot of extra time for the two of them.

Scratch that. Jim hadn't *wanted* to make time for them. He'd wanted time for himself. He'd wanted to play more golf and watch ESPN. Eagerly, he'd settled into a routine that involved his interests and his time schedule.

All the while, Daphne had let him, though now that he stopped and thought about it, Jim was sure he'd spied a look of hurt in her eyes when he'd informed her that he was booked solid all weekend and had no time for her.

Was it too late to try and change?

That dinner at The Cork sure had been a disaster. But Daphne shouldn't have kicked him out of the house. Now there was no way the two of them could patch things up, living apart the way they were.

Lord knew things hadn't been going too well, now that he was out on his own. The past week had been frustrating, to say the least.

Oh, he'd tried. He'd gone to his office every

morning, and even had lunch one day with his buddies. But they were talking about their wives and trips and grandchildren. At the moment, he had no wife, no trip planned, and way too much quality time with his grandchildren. His very sweet, tiny granddaughter had spit up all over his new suit.

Grandchildren weren't near as much fun when you couldn't give them back after a few hours.

To top that off, after four nights at Kevin's, he'd been dropped off like an unwanted houseguest at Jeremy's home.

Now he was really in no mood to be told what to do, or who to be nice to.

He didn't want to go visit Daphne and pretend to be interested in her flower garden just to be made to feel like he shouldn't have gone at all.

But Jeremy wasn't taking no for an answer. "Dad, I think you're making a mistake."

"I hear you." Before Jeremy could spout off any more advice, Jim stood up. "Do you have any more microwave popcorn? I think a couple of college games are on ESPN Classic and I could use a little snack."

With a frown, Jeremy said, "We're all out of popcorn. You ate the last of it last night."

"Really? Maybe you could—"

"Dad, you can't sit in here any longer."

Jim patted the couch like it was an old friend. "Sure I can. It's not the most comfortable piece of furniture in the world, but it should be just fine for a while."

Jeremy looked like he was about to snap. "I don't care about your comfort. It's almost six o'clock. 'Angeltubs' will be on."

Jim turned around. "Huh?"

" 'Angeltubs.' It's Bryan's favorite show. He watches it in here every night while Dinah makes dinner."

"Couldn't he watch it someplace else? I'm pretty settled."

"He's four."

"Where am I supposed to go?"

"To the flower show!"

Jim stood up. "Jeremy, I will get off this couch so Bryan can watch his show, but I am not going anywhere near your mother."

"Where are you going to go?"

"I'm going to go sit in my bedroom."

"And do what?"

Belatedly Jim realized there was no television in there. "I don't know. Read the paper. Call me when dinner is ready."

"No wonder Mom kicked you out." As Jeremy adjusted the television set, he said, "If Mom was here, she'd be helping with dinner."

"If your mother was here, I wouldn't be."

"Dad," Jeremy said after a long pause. "We're going to the club tomorrow night for dinner. Okay?"

Finally, something they could both agree on. "Sure. Tomorrow's Saturday night. It's Prime Rib Night."

"I knew you wouldn't forget that," Jeremy said just as Dinah opened the back door, Bryan racing ahead.

Jim closed his bedroom door just as Bryan threw himself at Jeremy's legs. "Daddy!"

Now alone, Jim sat down on his too-small bed and rested his head in his hands. Where had the time gone? It seemed like only yesterday that Jeremy had run to him and circled chubby arms around his knees. When there were designated TV nights for each kid. When music played out of kids' bedrooms too loud and too often.

When he and Daphne used to sit by the fire, and dream about their future. How they'd have hundreds of quiet nights together when the kids were finally gone.

But instead of a cozy fire, he was holed up in a tiny guest bedroom with only yesterday's newspaper for company.

Leaning back on the twin mattress, he frowned again. The mattress was as lumpy as Jeremy's couch. He made a mental note to tell Daphne that they ought to buy Jeremy and Dinah some furniture for Christmas before realizing he couldn't call her.

As he stared at the four walls surrounding him, Jim felt a lump in his throat.

What in the world had happened?

Chapter Eleven

For the first time in recent memory, Daphne was having a miserable time at the flower show. As she looked at all the beautiful bouquets of tea roses, lilies, and daffodils, it was all she could do to stifle a sigh.

Flowers just weren't cutting it anymore.

Actually, flowers were boring. Every single, stinking one.

Looking around, inhaling the too-sweet, cloying scent of the blasted freesia arrangement, Daphne wished she was anywhere else.

"Great show, Daphne!" Karen Anderson called out.

Daphne pasted a fake smile on. "Thanks, Karen."

"It's always a good show when you're in charge. Please tell me you're planning to head up this committee next year. If you didn't, we'd be devastated."

"You're too kind," Daphne replied, then turned away before Karen decided to come closer and chat.

That was the problem, now, wasn't it? For years, she would spend hours on committees and governing boards of different organizations. She could put together a dinner for four hundred in under four hours.

She could make a really spectacular table arrangement out of pinecones and apples.

She had a binder full of carefully preserved certificates of appreciation. But none of it mattered if Jim wasn't around to tell her he was proud.

And—Daphne was sorry to see—there was no Jim in sight. She knew he hated these shows. He didn't care for all the intricately decorated flower beds and the crowds of jabbering women.

But she'd still hoped that he would stop by and visit.

She was just remembering the last time he'd visited and she'd spent fifteen minutes lecturing him about the correct names for the perennials he'd liked when she was tapped on the arm.

"Excuse me, ma'am?"

"Yes?"

"Do you know where the information booth is? I have a couple of questions."

Daphne knew where the booth was. She'd manned it for years than she could count.

But there was something in the young woman's eyes that made her want to do more than just point to the small building around the corner. "I've worked here a number of years. I'm fairly knowledgeable about all of it. What may I help you with?"

The gal looked a little worried. "Oh. Well. I was actually looking for information about learning more about this club."

Daphne sneaked a better look at the young woman. Her shoes were scuffed and her light sweater was hopelessly stretched out of shape. "Do you garden?"

"Yes. Well, I hope to one day."

"Ah."

Obviously uncomfortable, the woman peered over Daphne's shoulder. "Um, I was just going to see if there was any registration forms."

"To join?"

Daphne knew she must have sounded surprised because the girl took two steps back. "It's okay. I—"

"No! Stay. I love to speak to anyone who's interested in horticulture."

"Well, that's me." Eyes lighting up, she added, "I like plants, you know?"

"I do know," Daphne said. She also knew that there was something about this woman that she liked.

Maybe it was because she looked in need of a friend?

Making a quick decision, Daphne said, "You know what? They serve sodas just a little bit to our right. How about we sit down and talk? I'll bring some brochures, too."

"You have time for that, ma'am?"

"I have nothing *but* time, dear."

Daphne spent the next two hours getting to know Jyl and eagerly learning about her life. Her parents divorced when she was young and neither parent had much time for her. Consequently, Jyl had a lot of goals, but no help to achieve them.

What this young woman needed, Daphne decided, was a friend who wanted to lend a guiding hand. Someone who had time to answer questions and was knowledgeable enough to be helpful.

She needed Daphne Reece.

When they parted, Daphne gave Jyl her phone number and strict instructions to call her soon so that she could come over and see Daphne's garden . . . and fill out the application for membership for the gardening club.

As she drove home and fought the Friday evening traffic, Daphne felt more optimistic than she had in a very long while.

Maybe her problem hadn't just been Jim. Maybe part of her discontent had been with her life.

With a feeling of surprise, Daphne realized that maybe Jim had been right!

As she pulled into her empty garage, she frowned as the stab of loneliness hit her hard again. She missed her husband.

From what the kids had said, he missed her, too. Maybe she should give him a call, just to see how he was doing—to see if he was remembering to eat his whole grains and lay off the fried eggs.

Then, if things were going pretty good, she could ask him over for lunch. She could make BLT's, just how he liked, with the turkey bacon. Then, over tall glasses of iced tea, they could iron out their disagreements. She could tell him about her new idea for a job and see what he thought about that.

Just thinking about having Jim back made Daphne smile.

Chapter Twelve

It was nights like this when Ginny longed for a mother. Someone to call and ask about what to wear to country clubs. Someone to go shopping with. But, as she stood in front of her closet and found nothing that looked cute, she shrugged.

Once again, she was totally on her own.

She'd once read in a fashion magazine that when in doubt, always choose black. After sorting through a myriad of outfits only suitable for teaching small children, she spied the black cocktail dress she'd bought years ago. She pulled it out and examined it critically. The knee length concoction hung limp and dusty on a wire hanger.

Ginny held it in front of her, wrinkling her nose. No wonder she never wore it. Wearing black made her think of funerals, which made her think of her parents' funeral, which made her think that bad things can always happen.

Karma wasn't a good thing. Hastily, she returned the dress into the back of the closet, reminding herself to give it away as soon as possible.

The doorbell's chime was a welcome distraction. After tightening her robe's sash and looking through the peep hole, Ginny smiled. Daphne Reece was standing outside.

"Mrs. Reece, come on in."

"Thanks, dear." She scanned Ginny's attire. "I hope I didn't come at a bad time."

"No, not at all. Guess what? Luke asked me out to dinner. We're going to the Payton Country Club."

"He did? Well, my goodness. I'm going there tonight, too." Daphne narrowed her eyes at Ginny for a moment longer. "What are you going to wear?"

"I don't know. I was just attempting to sort through all that when you knocked. You've been there before, right?"

"A time or two."

"Do you have any ideas?"

Daphne walked right into Ginny's bedroom, talking all the while. "Let's see. It's Prime Rib Night, so anything goes."

Prime Rib Night didn't sound very romantic.

Her thoughts must have shown brightly because Daphne chuckled. "You'll enjoy the dinner, I promise. It's all very good. Well, it is if you like beef and potatoes." Her voice faltering, Daphne concluded, "Jim just loves Prime Rib Night."

Hoping to distract Daphne, Ginny pulled her toward her closet. "I don't have many too many things besides jeans and sweats, or teacher clothes. But if you see anything that might do the trick, please let me know."

"Black's always good."

Ginny was positive she did not want to pull out that cocktail dress again. "I don't wear black."

Daphne blinked. "Guess what? I don't either!" Like they were part of a secret club, she hooked her arm through Ginny's. "Let's see here. We want something sexy and cute." After scanning through her parade of clothes, she snapped her fingers. "Here we go. This is it!"

Ginny stared at the beige and ivory pantsuit she'd bought on sale and had never worn, since all daycare providers knew better than to ever, ever wear ivory. It also was a silky material that clung to her figure and made Ginny feel a little self-conscious. "Wow. I'd forgotten I'd had this."

"You'll look lovely, dear."

Ginny heard a despondent tone and felt guilty for only thinking of herself. "Come on into the living room. I'm sorry, I've been so worried about what to wear that I completely forgot to ask why you stopped by."

"I'm here for a couple of reasons," Daphne said, gracefully walking the few short steps to the couch. "First of all, I just wanted to see how you were doing."

"I'm fine."

"Good." Daphne took a deep breath. "Next . . . I also wanted to hear your opinion about an organization I'm thinking of starting. It's for women who are on their own and need a helping hand. I'm hoping to provide a support system for them." Biting her lip, she said, "Do you think women out on their own would be receptive to help from . . . strangers?"

Ginny smiled to herself. Remembering how alone she'd felt when she graduated high school, she said, "I think so."

"I was hoping you would say that. I want to help women in need, but I don't want to be overwhelming." Straightening her shoulders, she murmured, "I have a tendency to go at things full throttle. I, uh, don't know if you've noticed that."

"I've noticed that a time or two." As she thought of everything that had happened to her since she answered the ad for the apartment, Ginny wondered how to best describe the wealth of gifts Mrs.

Reece had given her. "You've done so much for me, done so many things I didn't even think I needed."

"Really?"

Ginny nodded. "You've rented me an affordable place to stay. You introduced me to Luke. You've given me your time and your patience and your wisdom. And, through it all, you've made me feel important. That's a gift, Daphne. You should definitely use that gift to help other women."

Daphne's expression softened. "I can't tell you how good that makes me feel. The thing I enjoy most is helping people. Being supportive."

"You're great at that. I think you should begin your program."

"I was hoping you'd say that." Daphne looked at her sideways. "See, I really miss my kids needing me. Do you think that's awful?"

"I don't think so."

"I miss being involved in their lives. I've never wanted to run them . . . but I sure wanted to be a part of them. Now that they're all grown up, they don't need me. I pretended I didn't care, but actually, Ginny, I think I did. I do."

"What about Mr. Reece?"

"Oh, him?" Tears pricked Daphne's eyes. "I miss Jim so much. I hope he misses me, too."

"I bet he does," Ginny said with conviction. How could he not?

"I should have never left that restaurant in a huff instead of trying to work things out. Now everything's messed up. The kids are about to kill Jim, he's driving them so crazy. Everyone is miserable." She sighed in despair. "I've been trying to gather up my courage to call him, but I'm afraid he won't want to talk to me." Shoulders slumping, Daphne added, "It's a real mess."

"Things will get better soon. They always do."

Brightening, Daphne nodded. "You're right." Daphne gave Ginny a fierce hug. "I'm so glad you answered that ad in the paper about renting this apartment. What would I do without you?"

"I'd miss you, too," Ginny whispered.

After visiting for a few more minutes, she walked Daphne to the door. "I'll see you at the club," she said simply. "And, thanks for the help with the outfit."

"Wear your hair down, dear. It will look beautiful." Then, in a flash, Daphne Reece was gone.

"Tell me how you became a member of the Payton Country Club," Ginny said once she'd buckled up and Luke had pulled his Ford Explorer away from the curb.

"Well, you know how I told you I went to school with Kevin Reece?"

"Yes."

"We've stayed in touch. Actually, his company has been great supporters of the local police. One year they sponsored a silent auction to help the police and fire department. The manager of the club, Payton Chase, offered a membership as one of the prizes. I bid and won." Chuckling, he added, "I never thought I'd want to be part of the country club set, but I've found I enjoy it from time to time. And, it does give me a chance to wear something besides jeans on my days off."

Ginny thought Luke looked very neat and successful. Before, she'd only seen him in his uniform or jeans. His tailored tweed blazer and dress pants fit him very well, and his tie, in its shades of blue, teal, and brown, off-set the color of his eyes and hair. "How often do you go?"

"Not so much. I've never been one for golf, but I like going to these buffets. Payton Chase has been kind enough to let me continue being a member, paying only the social dues. It's a lot more affordable than paying what the golf members do."

To Ginny, Luke might as well been speaking Chinese. Tennis courts, social gatherings, and monthly dues for private memberships were completely out of her realm.

She began to be nervous. What if their differences were going to be even more pronounced when they arrived? Maybe Luke would see her falter about which fork to use, or be put off when he saw she didn't know how to act around rich people.

Taking hold of her hand when they arrived, Luke said, "I'm sure you're going to have a good time tonight."

"Well, I am hungry."

Luke laughed. "Good."

As they walked up the stairs of the white pillared building, Ginny heard a lot of commotion from within. Luke paused as he opened the door. "I wonder what's going on."

When they entered, Ginny saw an extremely well-tailored man at the podium at the entrance to the restaurant looking terribly agitated. Angry voices echoed in the distance.

Luke stepped forward, his fingers still entwined with hers. "What's going on, Payton?"

"What's not?" Turning to Ginny, he held out his hand. "Hi. Payton Chase."

"Ginny Young," she said, shaking his hand before looking curiously into the restaurant.

Obviously agitated, Payton said, "Luke, you might want to go get a drink in the bar for a little bit. Things are crazy in the dining room."

"What happened?"

"The Reeces are here."

"That's not news. Which ones?"

"Every stinking one."

A rush of raised voices rose and fell through the room like a tidal wave. Payton glared toward the dining room.

Luke laughed. "I've never known them to be so loud."

As two couples left, one elderly woman glaring at Payton, he shook his head. "I never have, either. It's ugly in there."

As the voices rose, Payton cringed.

Luke stepped forward. "How about I see if I can help you out a little?"

"You'd have to gag multiple family members to do that. Personally, I don't think you'd stand a chance. It's practically a full-out war in there."

Another couple came out, this one stopping at the podium. After a perfunctory nod at Luke, the blustery man turned to Payton. "Go stop this, Chase. That constant bickering spoiled my appetite."

"Mr. McKinley, maybe you should say something to them," Payton said hopefully. "After all, you've been friends with Jim and Daphne for decades."

"Not long enough to do what needs to be done,"

Baron McKinley replied with a frown. "They need a good kick in the pants."

Payton groaned. "I can't do that."

"You better do something, Chase. I'm on the board of directors. We hired you to manage this place, not wander around, twiddling your thumbs."

Unexpectedly, Luke was treated to a glare of his own. "You! Keep the peace!"

Luke visibly grimaced as Baron and Marianne McKinley marched out. "Yikes," he said to Payton. "You've got your hands full."

"You don't know the half of it. Nobody's eating, people are ignoring the buffet, and a couple of people have threatened to hire a new manager if I can't control Jim and Daphne."

Ginny was horrified. "They can't do that."

"You'd be surprised about what this crowd thinks they can and can't do." Peeking around the corner, at the buffet that no one was touching, Payton added, "More than a few people have come in, heard the commotion, and turned right around. We're going to have mountains of food left over. Tonight's going to be a total wash."

The manager, for all of his good looks, looked miserable. Ginny felt sorry for him. She shifted uncomfortably and tried to catch Luke's attention. Maybe they should go, too?

When their eyes met, Luke reached out and squeezed her shoulder. "I'm sorry, Ginny. I promise this is not what I intended for this evening."

"It's never like this," Payton added. "At least not since I've been the manager."

If anything, the commotion and entertaining cast of characters had lifted Ginny's mood. No, she wasn't rich and had never had even a minute's worth of etiquette classes, but she did have experience with arguing families and siblings. "It's okay."

Luke stepped back. "Maybe we can try The Cork? It's kind of fancy, but I bet—"

"You're not going to leave me here all alone, are you?" Payton interrupted.

"I hate to break it to you, but this wasn't what was on our agenda tonight, either, Payton."

Payton glanced toward the restaurant, a look of optimism in his eyes. "Things are sure to calm down soon. Why don't you two go have a drink in the bar for a few minutes? Maybe you should stay. The desserts are especially good tonight . . . and plentiful since everybody's leaving early."

Voices rose again. When another couple scurried out the doors, chiding Payton as they did so, he looked like he'd had about all he could take.

Turning to Ginny and Luke, Payton said, "The way I see it, I've got two options. I can either tell the whole Reece clan to leave, which will do me long-term harm because every one of those Reeces comes here on a regular basis. Or I can ignore them, which will also do me harm, because all of the other members will be wondering why I'm showing favoritism."

After winking at Ginny, Luke stepped toward the door. "How about I go in and see if I can help you out?"

"I hate to ask you to do that. But would you?"

"It's because of you that I have a membership here. I haven't forgotten. Of course I can." He turned to Ginny. "I should have asked. Is this okay with you?"

"I'm fine," Ginny said. She'd never admit it, but she was actually really looking forward to seeing how Luke was going to handle the dining crisis.

Eagerly, Payton stepped from out behind the podium and led both Luke and Ginny to the door of the restaurant. "I hate to make you work on your night off, but I'd really be grateful for anything you can do."

"I'll do my best."

"If you get them to leave, I'll comp your dinner. The next one, too."

With an embarrassed glance at Ginny, Luke shook his head. "That's not necessary."

"It would be my pleasure. Believe me, I'm

willing to do whatever I can to restore order around here."

Luke patted Payton on the shoulder. "I'll go see what I can do." He paused before stepping into the fray. With a frown, he turned to Ginny. "Would you like to go wait in the bar? It might be safer."

"And miss my new favorite family going at it? Miss my favorite police officer in action, keeping the peace? Not a chance."

"All right, then." With a sigh, Luke strode forward. "I'm going in."

Chapter Thirteen

Ginny burst out laughing when she saw what awaited them.

The Reece family was definitely hard to miss.

A crowd of beautifully dressed Reeces were seated at two central tables, each member looking both horrified and amused at the same time. Mr. and Mrs. Reece were standing, seemingly oblivious to the scene they were making.

Though Ginny didn't know some of the members of the clan, she couldn't help but be surprised at some of the younger Reeces' expressions.

Joanne, who'd always looked like she never was afraid to say what was on her mind, had her head on an extremely handsome man's shoulders. Denise looked resigned to having a miserable time and was playing tic-tac-toe with a guy in a denim shirt and down-home good looks. Even Kevin, who by all accounts was the head of the kids and the all-around even-tempered one, looked ready to run out of the restaurant.

The rest of the group looked irritated and at their wits' end.

Seated at several other tables were a couple of other diners, their plates full. No one seemed to be doing anything other than watch Daphne and Jim Reece throw insults at each other.

"Enough is enough," Luke said, motioning for them to sit. "Okay, everyone. It's time to relax and take your seats."

Immediately, every eye in the restaurant turned to him. Luke stood firm, showing no hesitancy at all.

Jim Reece screwed up his face as he stared at Luke in shock. "What?"

Luke stopped at the head of the table. "You all are disturbing the peace."

Jim Reece glared toward the restaurant's entrance, where Payton was lurking. "Chase, did you call the police on us?"

Payton darted from view.

With admirable patience, Luke tried again. "Jim. Daphne. Take your seats and lower your voices."

Daphne propped her hands on her hips. "Listen,

here, Luke. I'm well past the age of having someone like you telling me to remember my table
manners."

"Daphne. Take. Your. Seat."

Perversely, Daphne Reece stood a little
straighter. "I think you are being a little over-
eager, don't you think?" Seeing Ginny, who'd just
taken a seat of her own at one of the vacant tables
nearby, she gave a little wave. "Oh, hi there,
Ginny! How's the date going?"

Joanne glared her mother. "Mom. Be quiet."

"I will not."

Two Reece kids groaned.

Luke leaned down to Kevin. "What happened?"

"Neither Dad nor Mom knew the other one was
going to be here. They didn't take the news well."

Luke glanced toward Cameron. "Payton is
about to have a conniption fit out in the foyer. He's
losing customers. People are complaining. This
isn't the place for these antics."

Kevin's gray eyes blinked twice. "You don't
think I know that?"

"If they won't settle down, your parents need to
leave."

With a tired look at the rest of his siblings,
Kevin grunted. "We've tried. Lord, we've tried."

"Okay."

Winking at Ginny, Luke strode forward. "Jim,

Daphne, perhaps you could come over and sit with me for a minute."

Jim sputtered. "Now, listen—"

"Only for a moment. I promise."

As Ginny watched, Luke escorted Mr. and Mrs. Reece to a back table.

Visibly, everyone else's moods in the room brightened.

"Halleluiah!" Joanne said. "I think this calls for a bottle of wine."

"I'll second that," a pretty gal with short brown hair said.

Denise motioned to Ginny. "Come join us, Ginny."

Ginny wasn't sure if she should or not. "I'm okay."

"Please, do," Joanne added. "Take my mom's spot." When Ginny got up to join them, Joanne kept chattering. "Thank goodness you and Luke showed up. Or did Payton call the police?"

"No. Luke's off-duty now, anyway. We were here for dinner."

Kevin Reece leaned forward. "I'm so sorry our parents ruined your evening."

Ginny couldn't lie. "It's been kind of fun, seeing Luke in action."

"It's actually been kind of fun seeing my parents lose it," Joanne exclaimed. "You don't know how many times I've wondered how come I have such a hard time in social situations."

"We've all gotten hours and hours of relation-ship advice," Denise added. "Though it helped, I never thought our parents would ever be anything but extremely happy with each other."

"When Stratton and I were dating, I kept think-ing I'll never have what Mom and Dad have," Joanne said.

"Now I see that we've had it all along," Stratton, her husband teased.

"They meddle in everything. It's good for them to get a taste of their own medicine," Cameron added. "Ah, terrific. Here's the wine. Payton, thanks."

Payton looked worriedly over at Jim and Daphne. "I hope things are getting better over there."

They all turned to see Daphne and Jim glaring at Luke like he'd crashed their birthday party.

Denise shook her head. "You better bring over another bottle, Payton. Things might not be better for a while."

Chapter Fourteen

Daphne could not believe she was getting chastised by a man young enough to be her son.

And what was ten times worse—everything he said was completely true.

"I suggest you two go home and take care of this in a more private manner. If you don't feel that you can talk this out calmly, I can give you several phone numbers of capable counselors."

Jim looked affronted. "Luke, we don't need counseling."

"Then why were you two creating such a scene?" Sitting across from them, Luke continued. "I've known you both for most of my life. The behavior you two are displaying tonight is disgraceful. Payton is losing business. Friends and colleagues of yours are running out of here because you both are so unpleasant to be around."

Daphne swallowed hard. Luke was right.

Luke continued. "Payton even asked me to step in. Not as a member, but because I'm a police officer." He glared at them both. "Don't you think things need to change immediately?"

Jim, a stain of red on his cheeks, glanced toward Daphne. "I saw Baron and Marianne leave."

"People are going to be gossiping about this for weeks," Daphne said, with a gasp. Now she felt even more appalled. All her life she had done her best to make sure she kept a stellar reputation. All those years of hard work were being erased in a heartbeat.

Luke leveled a look toward her, reminding Daphne of the time she'd gotten sent to the principal's office in third grade for saying a bad word. She felt just as ashamed and disgraceful. "Daphne, your children are embarrassed. They don't know what to do."

Daphne gasped. In all the excitement, she hadn't even thought about how all five of her children must have felt, watching their parents lose it in front of the whole community.

"I heard one of them tell Ginny that he's never seen you two act like this," Luke added.

Jim shrugged. "We haven't."

"We've always been very happy," Daphne added tentatively. "Right, Jim?"

Glumly, Jim nodded.

Luke leaned forward. "So . . . what happened?"

Helplessly, Daphne turned to Jim. "I'm not sure anymore. Do you know?"

"All I know is that I was listening to music for thirty years that I now know you hate."

"I never hated classical music," she admitted. "I never realized you hated all the clubs and organizations I've been a part of."

"I never hated those."

"But don't you think they're a waste of time?"

Jim shook his head slowly. "Never. Daphne, a day doesn't go by that someone doesn't stop and tell me what a good friend you've been to them, or how their group is better off because you've put your leadership skills behind it."

"You've never told me that."

"Not lately." Jim wrinkled his nose. "I thought you knew it."

"I wouldn't have minded hearing it again."

"I wouldn't have minded if you told me you were glad I was around so much. Sometimes I feel like you resent me being home."

"I could never resent that, Jim. You've worked hard all of your life."

"But you never acted happy to see me."

"I thought you knew. I was always happy to see you. I always had dinner made and did my best to have the house welcoming."

"I always appreciated that," Jim said. "I miss being home with you."

"Now that you're semi-retired, I've loved having you home more," Daphne admitted, surprising herself with how much she meant her words. "I just wanted to feel like you were happy to be with me, too. It's been lonely without you."

"I love being with you. I hate living with the kids," Jim admitted after darting a look at their assorted offspring. "I liked seeing them for short amounts of time."

With a chuckle, he said, "This morning, I had to stop myself from telling Jeremy to stack in his dishes. The last thing I want to worry about in my life is whether Jeremy washes out his cereal bowl."

"Oh, Jim."

Luke glanced at toward the other people in the dining room. "Let's wrap this up."

"In a minute, Luke," Jim said, holding out a hand to Daphne. "I'm so glad to see you, and that we've been clearing everything up. I thought you wanted space from me."

"We know that isn't true."

"I thought you wanted to go out carousing around town without me."

"Oh, Jim. You know I don't carouse." Daphne squeezed her husband's hand. When it gripped hers, feeling strong and warm and so very familiar, she sighed. "I've missed you."

Jim leaned forward. "I've missed you too, Bunny."

"Bunny?" Luke shot up. "I think I'll go now."

Daphne turned to him right before her lips met Jim's. "Thanks, Luke."

Luke fought a shiver as he went to claim Ginny. All five of the Reece kids and their five spouses clapped when he returned.

"Is everything okay now?" Cameron asked

Luke fought a smile. "I believe so."

"Oh my gosh," Joanne gasped. "Mom and Dad are making out in the booth. We can't take them anywhere."

Luke started laughing. Ginny reached for his hand. "What's so funny? I was watching you. One moment you were sitting there, looking like you were giving them a piece of your mind, the next, you were hightailing it over here.

Luke only had one word to say to that. "Bunny."

All five Reece faces grew bright red.

"What in the world does that mean?" Dinah Reece, Jeremy's wife said.

"Bunny is my father's pet name for our mom,"

Jeremy explained. "Personally, I could have gone all my life without hearing him call her that again."

All kids glanced at their parents again, who seemed to be oblivious to the fact that they were in a public place, that their children were all watching them, or that they were near sixty years old.

Missy smiled at Jeremy. "I think it's sweet how in love they are. I think 'Bunny' is awfully cute. Don't you, Stratton?"

With a broad smile, Stratton replied, "Cute as all get out."

"Ugh." Joanne shivered. "He only calls her Bunny when they think they're alone."

Kevin glanced toward his parents again. "Oh, honestly. They're still kissing. Payton's going to ban our family from this place."

Cameron grabbed his wife's hand. "Sit down and join us, Luke. We took a vote. We need a break from Mom and Dad. You two come have some wine and dinner with us."

Warily, Luke glanced toward Ginny. "What do you want to do?"

"You saved the day, Luke," she said with a laugh. "I'd love to join the Reece family, if you're sure it's okay."

"Please join us," Kevin said, still warily eyeing his parents. "If our parents, uh, finish soon, we're sending them home."

"To their *own* house," Jeremy added.

And because Luke couldn't help but rib the guy a little, he said, "Your dad said you have a real problem with not washing your own dishes."

Jeremy groaned. "Cameron, next time Dad and Mom break up, you're taking Dad."

Cam glanced over at his parents. "By the looks of things, I think I'm safe for the time being."

The whole table burst into laughter.

Chapter Fifteen

"This had to be one of the strangest nights of my life," Ginny said as they hopped in Luke's car. "I had no idea such a big family could inspire so much drama."

"This was excessive, even for the Reeces," Luke admitted. "I'm just sorry our evening didn't turn out like I'd hoped."

"It wasn't so bad."

"It wasn't so good." Taking Ginny's hand, he said, "First, I was going to let you be wowed by my membership in such a swanky club."

The reality of what had happened was so completely different, Ginny chuckled. "And then?"

"Then, after having a wonderful dinner by candlelight, I was going to ask if you'd like to go for a drive. You, in a cosmic daze after eating delicious food, would instantly agree."

"I did agree to eat with you," she pointed out. "I could still be persuaded to go for a drive, well, if it wasn't so late."

Luke squeezed her hand. "That's good news. Maybe we'll do that tomorrow night."

Ginny leaned a little closer. "What did you want to happen, during our drive?"

"I wanted you to enjoy the cool evening, and be able to listen to me for what I want to say next."

"Which is?"

"I think we're pretty good together."

"I agree."

"But . . . I'm not going to change occupations, even though I know you're not comfortable around cops. I'm not going to quit the police force, Ginny."

Shocked, she dropped his hand. "I don't want you to."

"Are you sure? I don't want my job to come between us . . . but I don't want us to interfere with my career."

Touched by his sensitivity, she clasped his hand. "Thank you for bringing this up. But my perspective on police has changed since we first met."

He cocked an eyebrow. "You think so?"

"Definitely." Hoping to try and convey her

thoughts, Ginny said, "A couple of weeks ago, when you helped me with the break-in, I saw a whole different part of your job. You made me see that first of all, police can really do some good."

"And secondly?"

"I wasn't being fair by classifying you only for your occupation. There's a lot more to you than your job, just like there's a whole lot more to me than teaching preschool."

Luke visibly relaxed.

Encouraged, Ginny bared her heart. "But what really made me want to spend time with you is what happened tonight."

"What did I do?"

"You handled Mr. and Mrs. Reece like their problems were worth your time, even though no crime had been committed. You helped them finally sit and talk. And you helped Payton, who looked like he really, really needed you. Finally, you helped the kids . . . and you didn't have to do a thing, Luke."

"All my police work isn't like this," he warned. "I still do traffic stops. I still investigate robberies and other crimes."

"I know that. But I've decided that I like being around a person who enjoys helping others. It makes me want to trust other people, too."

"You should. If you'd open your eyes, you'd see

that there are lots of people in this town who want to be your friend."

"I'll take that, as long as you're with me, too."

"Yeah?"

"Yeah. I like you, Luke." As she heard her voice echo in the confines of his car, Ginny felt her cheeks heat. Gosh, could she sound any more juvenile?

But the smile on Luke's face dispelled all her insecurities. "I've been hoping you'd say that, soon. I can't tell you how happy this makes me."

"Me too," Ginny announced. "In fact, only one thing could make me happier."

Chuckling, Luke glanced at her sideways. "What is that?"

"If you pulled over soon."

His body tensing, Luke looked around in surprise. "What's wrong?"

"I want to kiss you, silly. Even I don't want Payton, Ohio's favorite police officer to get in trouble for not paying attention to the road."

Taking her hand again, Luke did two quick right turns, followed by a leisurely left along a windy farm road. Finally, he pulled into a small park, where the parking spaces were partially obscured by over-hanging trees. "How's this?"

Unbuckling her seatbelt, Ginny smiled. "Perfect. How did you know this was here?"

Luke unbuckled his own, then pulled her onto his lap, so that her back was against his door and her feet were setting on her seat. "Because, Ginny Young, I was not always a cop."

And then finally his lips claimed hers. And the sparks that flew between them were as bright and vibrant as any fireworks show in the sky.

Two weeks passed. School was out for the summer, the balmy nights had been replaced by hot and humid evenings, and, finally, everyone in Payton had settled into barbecues, lawn parties, canoeing on the river, and enjoying the not-too-hot temperatures of June.

Ginny knew she would always remember the past month as a wonderful, amazing, terrific one. So much had happened. Mr. and Mrs. Reece, after making up in the country club's dining room, went home together, much to the relief of everyone involved.

James, the boy who had broken into Ginny's apartment, wrote her a note of apology. His parents wrote a note and a sizable check to help pay for Ginny's losses.

Ginny and Luke saw each other every day. Ginny knew things between them were getting serious. So serious, she'd contacted Daphne and scheduled a meeting with her at the Payton Mill coffee shop. Ginny hoped to hear some advice regarding things with Luke and to broach a subject that made her uncomfortable.

As she made her way to the appointment, Ginny's stomach was a jumble of knots. After everything Daphne Reece had done for her, Ginny hoped she wouldn't come across as ungrateful.

The Mill was crowded when she entered, but Daphne, as usual, was easy to spot. Today she was wearing a stylish flowing coral skirt and matching jean jacket. Chunky gold earrings adorned her ears. And a brilliant smile lit up her face when she spotted Ginny.

"I'm so glad you wanted to meet, dear," Daphne said after they waited in line and purchased cups of steaming gourmet coffee and cinnamon scones. "Everything's been so crazy, what with my new job and all, I've hardly had time to catch up with you."

"Things have been busy with me, too. After the school year ended, I had lots of meetings to plan next year . . . and I've been spending almost every minute with Luke."

"I'm glad to hear that, especially since I was the one who introduced the two of you." With a satisfied smile, Daphne leaned back and smiled. "I can't tell you how glad I am to hear that you're happy."

The knot in her stomach seemed to double and triple in size. As she sipped on her coffee, Ginny realized it was going to be even tougher to break the news than she'd originally thought.

Daphne stabbed at her scone with a fork. "Hold on, now. Something's not as 'great' as you're leading me to believe. What is it?"

Daphne's penetrating stare felt like a laser. "I—see, it's like—"

"Spit it out, dear."

Caught off guard by hearing Daphne utter such a thing, Ginny said, "I want to move. I know I signed my lease at the apartment for a year, but I don't think I can live there much longer."

Daphne carefully put her fork down. "Oh. Hmm."

Ginny rushed on before she lost her nerve. "It's not that I don't appreciate everything you've done for me. I do. And the apartment really is cute. I'm just not comfortable there."

"Because of the break-in?"

"Partly. But, it's mainly because of the ghost. I don't know if it's really haunted, or just really old, but living there creeps me out, Daphne. Now that I'm home from school, it's bothering me even more."

To her surprise, Daphne chuckled. "I imagine living there would creep me out, too." After taking another bite of the treat, she drummed her fingers on the table. "Hmm. I wonder what to do with the place now."

"You don't seem surprised."

"Oh, I'm not." With a dramatic shudder, Daphne said, "I wouldn't want to live there. And, now that I think about it, Lindsay wasn't a fan of living in that apartment, either." Daphne cocked her head. "Actually, the only one who enjoys the stories of the ghost is Denise, and she moved out as soon as she could."

Now her dirt-cheap rent made a lot more sense. "I didn't realize it was a hard place to keep occupied."

"Oh, yes. That's why I ended up putting an ad in the paper. Denise had given up ever renting it out and was going to leave it empty, but I was sure I could find somebody willing to live there."

"Me."

Daphne brightened. "Exactly! And thank goodness you moved here. Otherwise we would have never met, I would have never started Friends Helping Friends and poor Luke would still be all alone."

Ginny wasn't quite sure that she was responsible for all the events, but she wisely stayed silent on that. "So, you're not mad?"

"Not at all."

"I'm glad."

"Where are you planning to live? You're not going to move from Payton, are you?"

"Oh, no. Things with Luke and me are going great. So well, I'm reluctant to sign another one-year lease, just in case we get even more serious. When I mentioned it to Joanne, she asked if I would live with her and Stratton and Eric and help out."

"I can understand that. Stratton is extremely busy, being the town's favorite physician and all. Joanne's job is a demanding, too. Now that I'm occupied with my own projects, I can't baby-sit all the time."

Ginny hid a smile. "No, ma'am."

"Well, I'll go ahead and talk to Denise this weekend when she comes over for Sunday dinner. We'll figure something out." She stirred her coffee. "In the meantime, tell me all about you and Luke and your plans for the rest of the summer."

Finally relaxing, Ginny did just that. She smiled with Daphne as she shared stories about Luke's latest investigation and the camp she taught at the nearby YMCA.

In turn, Daphne filled Ginny in on her mentoring program and her Sunday drives with Jim.

As they talked, Ginny waved to several people who entered the Mill that she knew. She shook hands with the dozen other man and women

Daphne introduced her to. In short, she felt comfortable and happy. Like she belonged in Payton.

Which, of course, had been the reason she moved there in the first place.

How nice to find out that sometimes everything in the future really does go as planned.

Epilogue

"Well, this is a nice surprise, Jim," Daphne said as she entered the kitchen to find Jim already there, wearing a *Warning: Men Cooking* apron and looking extremely industrious.

He beamed. "I'm barbecuing. All the kids are coming over."

Daphne racked her brain, but no special occasion came to mind. September was usually their quiet month, before the storm of October birthdays and then the hustle and bustle of the holiday season. "Everyone?"

"Yep. Hand me a towel, would you hon? I've managed to get sauce and seasoning over half the counter."

As she did so, Daphne noticed a couple more

things. Stacks of paper plates, plastic silverware, and cups were stacked neatly on the kitchen table. Sacks from the country club were on the floor. She walked over to inspect them, only to find they were empty. "What did you get from the club?"

"Beans and potato salad. Oh, and two pies. Apple and cherry."

Now she was really confused. "What is going on? I never called the kids to—"

"Don't worry. Priscilla Chase at the club made everything. When I called her last week to talk about this dinner, she said it would be no problem. I picked them up about an hour ago. The beans are in the oven, staying warm."

Daphne hadn't known that Jim could work the oven, let alone prepare a whole dinner. Then what he said registered. "Last week? You've been planning this?"

"I did. Well, the kids helped. They're bringing stuff, too, so don't do a thing." As he continued to add spices to the tray of chicken, he said, "I'm going to go turn on the grill."

"When is everyone coming over?"

After he washed his hands, Jim looked at his watch. "In about fifteen minutes."

"Fifteen minutes! Jim, what were you thinking?"

"That the less amount of time you had to stress

about all this, the better. Why don't you get out of that suit and slip on some jeans, dear?"

With some dismay, Daphne realized she was wearing her new "power suit", the one she bought for her meetings at the board for Families Helping Families, the organization she helped found a couple of months ago.

Though things were moving slowly, word had gotten around of her group's mission, to help other families with dignity and friendship. So far they'd had eight applications for assistance.

Quickly, Daphne trotted upstairs, unbuttoning her blazer as she did so. Within minutes, she'd slipped on a cute pair of denim capris, some new turquoise sandals, and a matching blue, aqua, and pink striped sweater. She was just heading back down to interrogate Jim when the front door opened and Cameron, Mary Beth, and Maggie came in.

"Hi, Mom," Cam called out.

She rushed down the last four steps to meet them. "Cameron, did you know about this barbeque your dad's been planning?"

"Yep."

"It's all he's been talking about," Mary Beth added, juggling a large picnic basket. "He's really been on a roll."

Daphne hugged Maggie and was about to ask more questions when in walked Kevin, Missy, and Tam.

"Hi, Mom," Kevin said, reaching down to give her a kiss on the cheek.

"Kevin, I was just asking Cameron about your father. Something strange is going on with him." Lowering her voice, she added, "Your dad is outside grilling chicken. Don't you think that—"

Kevin cut her off. "Don't worry, Mom. I'll go help him."

Missy held up a sack to Mary Beth. "Want to help me in the kitchen? I've got everything we need."

Daphne was about to follow the women and their little girls when the door opened once again. She stayed put.

"Mom," Joanne said with a wide smile as she carried in little Eric on one hip. "Look at you. A regular greeting party." Stratton followed right behind, his arms loaded with a box and a large tote bag.

Daphne once again gave everyone a hug. "Kevin and Cameron are already here."

Joanne nodded. "Where's Dad?"

"Grilling outside." Before they could disappear, Daphne asked impatiently, "Want to tell me what's going on?"

With a mischievous smile, Joanne shook her head. "No."

"No, you don't know what's going on?"

"No, I don't want to tell you a thing." Juggling Eric again, she said, "We're going to go on back. Stay here, though. Jeremy was parking his car right as we were unloading."

Sure enough, before Daphne could shut the door, Jeremy, Dinah, and Bryan came roaring through. "Gma!" Bryan squealed, launching himself into her arms. His warm hug and wet kisses effectively cut off any questions.

After patting her on the shoulder, Jeremy said, "We'll talk in a minute, Mom. Stay here, though. I saw Denise and Lindsay driving up."

"Okay."

"I love your sandals," Dinah said as she walked by.

"Thanks," Daphne replied, eager to talk about how she'd gotten them on sale, but Dinah was already gone.

Daphne tried not to feel left out, especially since she knew she was the guest of honor for some reason. But as the voices from the kitchen grew louder and more animated, she couldn't help wanting to go be a part of it—whatever 'it' was.

But once again, before she could take two steps,

the door opened, this time bringing Denise, her husband Ethan, Ethan's sister Lindsay, and her husband Craig. All were bearing boxes and bags.

"Hi Mom," Denise said, looking so happy Daphne would swear she was glowing. "Looks like we're almost the last to arrive."

After hugging everyone, Daphne pointedly asked, "For what?"

"You'll see," Denise said. Looking at the other three. "We're just going to—"

"I know. Go join the others." As Daphne heard a high pitched squeal, followed by a burst of laughter, she pivoted on her very stylish heel. "I think I'll follow this time."

Lindsay's eyes widened. "Oh, Daphne, you can't!"

Mentally, Daphne reviewed who had arrived. Cameron, Kevin, Joanne, Jeremy, Denise, and finally Lindsay. That about covered it. "All kids are accounted for," she said just as the door opened one more time.

And in walked Ginny.

Unable to stop tears from pricking her eyes, Daphne laughed. Ginny's appearance had certainly changed since their first meeting outside the theater. Where once sadness filled her expression, she now moved with confidence.

She also was looking at Daphne with warmth

instead of wariness. "What a nice surprise," Daphne said, giving Ginny a hug.

"When Joanne asked Luke and me to attend, there was no way I could say no."

Sure enough, in walked Luke, also carrying a bag. After greeting him, Daphne eyed the door. "Luke, do you know if anyone else is coming over?"

"I don't know who's here, but I have a feeling we might be the last. There's a slew of cars in your driveway."

Gesturing to Luke, Ginny said, "We would have been here sooner, but Luke had a little situation come up at work."

"It couldn't be helped," Luke said with a shrug. "We better head on back."

As Ginny and Luke darted toward the kitchen, Daphne stood in the foyer, all alone once again. As she heard the sounds of all her children and spouses, and the welcome cries and laughter of her grandkids, emotion overwhelmed her.

She sat down on the bottom step of the stairs.

Where in the world had the time gone?

For years, their house had been the noisiest one on the block. Commotion had filled the air every waking minute: kids running, fighting, late for sports, hungry for meals.

Needing poster board for projects.

Needing bandaids for cuts.

Needing her, immediately.

Some days, she'd sat on this very step, dreaming of being like Jeanie on the old TV show. Oh, what she would have given to be able to blink everyone still for ten minutes of silence.

Then, in a strange twist of fate, she'd found herself missing everything she'd just years ago wished would end. The house had been too quiet. Too big. She'd had too little to do.

"Daphne? What are you doing in here?"

She couldn't help but smile as she noticed Jim's apron was now liberally stained with sauce. "Nothing. Just listening."

Surprising her, Jim sat down on the step beside her. Cocking his head, he smiled as they heard Joanne bossing Cameron around.

"Some things never change," Jim said.

Thinking of the last two months, Daphne disagreed. "Some things do."

Understanding filled his gaze. "That's a fact."

"Are you ever going to tell me what's going on?"

He tried to play coy. "Why do you think something's going on?"

"Jim. I love my children dearly, but even I don't expect them to come over all at the same time, bearing gifts."

"Well, now that I think about it, there might be something going on."

"What?"

"It's a surprise."

"I hate surprises," she said, hopping up.

Jim stilled her with a hand. "You *love* surprises. And this one, if I do say so myself, is a good one."

"How did you do everything?"

"I got on the phone and called the kids. They helped." A shadow entered his gaze. "A lot. Every one of them can plan a party like nobody's business. They're certainly your kids."

As the kitchen filled with raucous laughter, Daphne grabbed Jim's hand. "Can we go in now?"

"Let's see." Raising his voice, he said, "Kevin, can your mother come in?"

"You should be asking me, Dad," Joanne called out. "I'm in charge."

"Yeah, right," Jeremy protested.

"I'm the oldest," Kevin retorted through the closed door, sounding half his age.

"Well?" Jim asked, a little more loudly.

After much debating and laughter, Cameron opened the door. "Come in, Mom. We're ready."

With a hesitant, backward glance toward Jim, Daphne dropped her husband's hand and walked forward.

And then wished she had it back when she saw what her children had done.

"It's a surprise party, Gma!" Bryan called out. "S-pise!"

Everyone in the room laughed and echoed Bryan's sentiments. "S-pise!"

"Oh!" Daphne said. "Oh, my."

Streamers and balloons and presents covered a good half of the well-used kitchen table. On the island were Jim's baked beans, potato salad, and chicken. Next to them were an array of other salads and side dishes. Two pies rested on the range, along with the most beautiful three layer cake she'd ever seen.

"It's not my birthday," she said.

"Mom, we know when your birthday is," Jeremy chided. "This is a congratulations party for your new job."

The party made no sense. "But we already went out to dinner, two months ago. Doesn't everyone remember? I had mahi-mahi."

Joanne rolled her eyes. "We remember, Mom. We all got together and decided to have another party now that things are going so well."

"This is a better celebration than at any restaurant, anyway," Denise said. "This one's at home."

Daphne couldn't have stilled her tears if she'd tried. She loved having everyone there. "This is better," she admitted. "Thank you."

After another round of hugs, Jim took her hand

and led her to the table, where a chair had been wrapped in pink bunting. "Sit down, dear."

When Kevin placed a book wrapped in thick brown paper in her lap, she held it cautiously. "From you?"

"It's from all of us."

"But you all already gave me a gift, I'm sure of it. Remember the roses? They were American Beauties—"

"Open it, Mom," Cameron called out.

She tore open the paper like a child. "Oh!" she said, unable to say anything else, because the tears were now streaming down her face in earnest.

Denise knelt at her feet. "Remember the books you made for each of us when we graduated high school? The ones filled with all your memories of us?"

Daphne could only nod. She'd loved making those books, but had thought the kids had merely stuffed them in their closets.

"We got together and made one for you," Denise said, opening up the front cover.

"We each did a page," Kevin added. "We wrote down memories and found pictures of you and us."

"I scanned and copied them all," Missy said. "They're really cute."

Daphne looked at Jim. "Have you seen this?"

"Yep." Standing proudly, Jim said, "I did a page, too."

"You?" She didn't think Jim even knew where the photo albums were.

With shaking hands, she opened the cover. Sure enough, there on the first page was a photo of she and Jim on their second date. Another was of their wedding day. But her favorite was the last photo he chose to display. It was she and Jim, both looking exhausted and oh-so young. Surrounding them on the grass were five little children, each covered in mud.

Unable to help herself, Daphne burst out crying. "Oh, I loved that day."

"You kids were a mess," Jim scolded their kids, just like twenty years hadn't passed. "Your mother was covered in mud by the time she got you all clean."

"That day was great," Cameron announced. "We clobbered you, Jeremy."

"That's because I was the youngest. I always got clobbered."

"Wait a minute," Joanne interrupted. "You are remembering it all wrong. I was the one—"

Daphne sniffed as the kids rehashed that day. Just like she used to do, she zoned them out, choosing to remember instead.

Those times with the children had been wonderful. So was this moment. And she had a feeling tomorrow was going to be pretty good, too.

Funny, how a lifetime of memories could bring forth a feeling of optimism.

And right then, at that very moment, Daphne Reece realized she was probably the luckiest woman in the world. She'd been lucky enough to find love, years and years ago.

That love was still strong, still pliable, still steadfast.

Strong enough to last a lifetime.

To last forever.